W9-BZW-734

"I'm not sure what I would do without you. Thank you, Brody."

The way his name rolled off her tongue brought back all kinds of memories he didn't need to be thinking about right now. "I haven't done anything yet."

"Yes, you have. An hour ago I was afraid of my own shadow."

"And now?"

"I'm relieved you're here. You look good, Brody."

The warmth her words spread through his chest almost made him wonder if going to her place was a good idea. He was a grown man now. And he had desires to match.

"You do, too. Better than good." Brody took her hand in his, ignoring how right it felt there, and walked her to her vehicle.

TEXAS PREY

BARB HAN

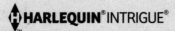

If you purchased this book without a cover you should be aware
that this book is stolen property. It was reported as "unsold and
destroyed" to the publisher, and neither the author nor the
publisher has received any payment for this "stripped book."

To Allison Lyons for the opportunity to learn so much with
every book. To Jill Marsal for unfailing wisdom and support.
To Brandon, Jacob and Tori for inspiration and kindness
(I love you!). To John for finding true love.

This story is as much about friendship as it is about love.
To Emily Martinez, Lisa Watson, Caroline York,
and Raymon and Amanda Bacchus for yours!

ISBN-13: 978-0-373-69858-5

Texas Prey

Copyright © 2015 by Barb Han

Recycling programs
for this product may
not exist in your area.

All rights reserved. Except for use in any review, the reproduction or
utilization of this work in whole or in part in any form by any electronic,
mechanical or other means, now known or hereinafter invented, including
xerography, photocopying and recording, or in any information storage
or retrieval system, is forbidden without the written permission of the
publisher, Harlequin Enterprises Limited, 225 Duncan Mill Road,
Don Mills, Ontario M3B 3K9, Canada.

This is a work of fiction. Names, characters, places and incidents are
either the product of the author's imagination or are used fictitiously,
and any resemblance to actual persons, living or dead, business
establishments, events or locales is entirely coincidental.

This edition published by arrangement with Harlequin Books S.A.

For questions and comments about the quality of this book,
please contact us at CustomerService@Harlequin.com.

® and TM are trademarks of Harlequin Enterprises Limited or its
corporate affiliates. Trademarks indicated with ® are registered in the
United States Patent and Trademark Office, the Canadian Intellectual
Property Office and in other countries.

Printed in U.S.A.

Barb Han lives in North Texas with her very own hero-worthy husband, three beautiful children, a spunky golden retriever/standard poodle mix and too many books in her to-read pile. In her downtime, she plays video games and spends much of her time on or around a basketball court. She loves interacting with readers and is grateful for their support. You can reach her at barbhan.com.

Books by Barb Han

Mason Ridge

Texas Prey

The Campbells of Creek Bend

Witness Protection
Gut Instinct
Hard Target

Harlequin Intrigue

Rancher Rescue

Harlequin Intrigue Noir

Atomic Beauty

CAST OF CHARACTERS

Rebecca Hughes—She escaped the man who abducted both her and her younger brother, Shane, fifteen years ago. She's never stopped searching for her baby brother. Now that the abductor is back, she'll have to rely on the only person she's ever been able to trust—Brody Fields.

Brody Fields—He's done his level best to forget the beauty from the past who still haunts his thoughts. And since that hasn't happened, he'll do whatever it takes to protect her and give her back the life that was stolen from her as a child.

Shane Hughes—His abduction fifteen years ago at age seven turned the small town of Mason Ridge upside down.

Randy Harper—Could he be the long-lost Shane? Or is it more dead ends and wishful thinking?

Ryan Hunt—His need to protect his big brother, Justin, was a habit formed in childhood. Has that same need driven him to overlook the fact that his brother and his friends might've been involved?

Justin Hunt—This older brother pulled himself out of a bad place with the help of his younger brother. Is he as innocent as he claims?

Gregory Hunt—This uncle was a prime suspect years ago but has since moved out of town and developed an even bigger drinking problem.

Charles Acorn—The richest man in the county has never been a fan of the Hunt family. In fact, he'd like nothing more than to see the whole lot behind bars.

Thomas Kramer—He's part of the breakdown crew for the Renaissance Festival that occupies Mason Ridge for a week every summer. Is he the key to finding Shane?

Lester Simmons—At first, he's written off as a man protecting his own by keeping vigilant watch of his fellow festival workers. Does he know more than he's letting on?

Sheriff Brine—He doesn't want to look back at his biggest career failure—allowing The Mason Ridge Abductor to get away.

Chapter One

Rebecca Hughes held her chin up and kept alert as she thrust her shopping cart through the thick, oppressive North Texas heat. She blinked against the relentless sun, a light so intense her eyes hurt.

The van parked next to her car in the grocery store lot pricked her neck hairs. Blacked-out windows blocked her view of the driver's side or anything else that might be lurking, waiting, ready. A warning bell wailed inside her head as she neared her sedan.

Today marked the fifteenth anniversary of that horrible day when both she and her younger brother were abducted, and it always put her on edge. The two had been isolated in separate sheds. When an opportunity had presented itself to run, Rebecca had escaped, thinking she could bring back help. Instead, she got lost in the woods and never saw her baby brother again.

Steering her cart toward the center of the aisle, she made sure no one could surprise her by jumping from between two cars. Tension squeezed her shoulder blades taut as memories assaulted her. Those thirty-six hours of torture before she escaped without her little brother, the horror and Shane's disappearance would haunt her for the rest of her life.

Shuddering at the memory, she tightened her grip on the handle and pushed forward. The early Friday-morning crowd was out. Most people were just beginning to run errands at the same time her workday ended. Her overnight shift at the radio station kept her sane after years of being afraid to be home alone in the dark.

She and Shane had been twelve and seven respectively when she'd sneaked out to play that stupid game with her friends. They'd been told to stay inside while the annual Renaissance Festival was in town, in full swing. Parents were busy, distracted. Strangers in costumes were everywhere. People came from nearly every state, descending on Mason Ridge in RVs and trailers and filling camp sites. And Shane was supposed to be asleep when she'd slipped out her bedroom window to meet up with her friends, not following her.

But none of that mattered. She should've realized sooner that the little stinker was trailing behind, his favorite blanket in tow. Shane had been her responsibility. And she'd let him down in the worst possible way.

The unfairness of his disappearance and her survival still hit with the force of a physical blow. His screams still haunted her. An imprint left by the horrible man who'd been dubbed the Mason Ridge Abductor was the reason she still watched every stranger warily.

When no one else had disappeared and all leads had been exhausted, law enforcement had written the case off as a transient passing through town. Logic said the man was long gone. Point being, he couldn't hurt her anymore. And yet, every time she got spooked he was the first person who popped into her thoughts. That monster had caused her to lose more than her sense of security. He'd shattered her world and taken away her ability to trust.

Her parents had divorced and become overbearing; friends looked at her strangely, as if she'd become an outcast; and she'd eventually pushed away the one person she'd truly loved—Brody Fields.

The van's brake lights created a bright red glow, snapping her focus to the present. Panic pressed heavy on her arms. Maybe she could circle around the next aisle and get back to the store before being seen.

There were a million wackos out there waiting to hurt unaware women, surprise being key to their attacks. Rebecca was fully present. She tightened her grip on the cart handle a third time, turned around and stalked toward her car. No one got to make her feel weak and afraid again.

Reaching inside her purse as she neared her vehicle, she gripped her Taser gun. Anyone trying to mess with her would get a big surprise and a few thousand volts of electricity. She wouldn't go down without a fight. Not again. She was no longer a shy twelve-year-old who could be overpowered in the dark.

With every forward step, the tension in Rebecca's body tightened. Her gaze was trained on the van.

She heard footsteps coming toward her from behind. Turning in time to catch a glimpse of a man rushing toward her, she spun around to face him. He was less than three feet away, moving closer. He wore a sweatshirt with the hood covering his hair and half of his face. Sunglasses hid his eyes. Before she could react, he slammed into her, knocking her off balance. She landed flat on the ground.

This time, she knew it was him—*had* to be him. She'd recognize that apple-tobacco smell anywhere. The scent had been burned into her senses fifteen years ago.

With the Taser already in hand, she struggled to untangle her purse strap from her arm. She shook free from his grasp, but not without upsetting the contents of her purse.

"You sick bastard. What did you do to my brother?" Aiming the blunt end of the Taser directly at his midsection, she fired.

The man fell to his knees, groaning, as she scrambled to her feet.

"What are you talking about, lady? You're crazy," he bit out through grunts and clenched teeth, convulsing on the ground.

Shaking off the fear gripping her, she snatched her handbag and ran to her car. She cursed, realizing some of the purse contents were on the ground. No way could she risk going back for them. Not with him there.

She hopped into the driver's seat, then closed and locked the door. Her fingers trembled, causing her to drop the keys. Scooping them off the floorboard, she tried to force a sense of calm over her.

Fumbling to get the key in the ignition, her logical mind battled with reality. That had to be *him*, right?

This wasn't like before when she'd mistaken one of the garbagemen for her abductor. Or the time she'd been certain he was posing as a cable guy. Anyone who'd come close and roughly matched her abductor's description had given her nightmares.

The sheriff had been convinced that no one from Mason Ridge was capable of doing such a horrific act. He'd said it had to be the work of a trucker or someone else passing through because of the festival. The FBI hadn't been so sure. They'd produced a list of potential suspects that had pitted neighbors and small-shop owners against one another. Personal vendettas had people coming forward.

As the investigation unfolded, there was no shortage of accused. And a town's innocence had been lost forever.

Determined investigators had traced freight cars and truckers that had passed through Mason Ridge the night both her and Shane had been abducted. In the days following, they'd scoured known teen hangouts, drained a lake and even set off dynamite in the rock quarry. But they'd come up empty.

They'd been reaching, just as she was now.

Guilt hit at the thought she could be overreacting. She'd never actually seen the face of the man who'd abducted them all those years ago. Had she just nailed a stranger with her Taser?

A quick glance in the side mirror said it didn't matter. This guy wasn't there to help with her groceries. The hooded man on the ground inched toward her, a menacing curve to his exposed lips, his body twitching.

She turned the ignition again with a silent prayer.

Bingo.

The engine cranked and she shifted into Reverse. Her tires struggled to gain traction as she floored the pedal. Fear, doubt and anger flooded her.

She checked the rearview again as she pulled onto the street. When she could be certain he wasn't following her, she'd pull over and call 911.

A few seconds later, she turned right onto the road and then made another at the red light, zipping into traffic at the busy intersection. A horn blared.

Adrenaline and fear caused her hands to shake and her stomach to squeeze. Tears stung the backs of her eyes. A couple more turns, mixing lefts and rights, and she pulled into a pharmacy parking lot. She reached for her purse, remembering that half the contents had spilled out in the

parking lot. Had any of her personal information fallen
out? On the concrete? Right next to him?

But it couldn't be *him*, could it?

Why would he come back after all these years?

The festival? The radio show? Every year she mentioned her brother near the anniversary of his disappearance and got threatening letters at the station. The
sheriff's office followed up with the same result as previous years, no enthusiasm, no leads.

Rebecca couldn't write it off so easily, had never been
able to. She scoured social media for any signs of Shane.
Last month alone, she must've sent a dozen messages to
people who matched Shane's description. Although she
still hadn't given up, her results weren't any better than
the sheriff's. But her resolve was.

Maybe it was her own guilt that kept her searching. Or,
a deep-seated need to give their mother closure.

Rebecca rummaged through her bag, desperate to locate her cell, and found nothing. It must've fallen out of
her purse. The sheriff's office was nearby. She'd have to
drive to the station to file a complaint against her attacker.
She cursed. No way could she get there in time for them
to take her information and then catch him. He'd be long
gone, most likely already was. She fisted her hand and
thumped the steering wheel.

If her on-air mention of Shane hadn't rattled any
chains, the media might have. Every year before the festival the local paper ran some kind of article referenc-
ing Shane's disappearance. This year being the fifteenth
anniversary had brought out the wolves. A reporter had
been waiting in the parking lot at work two weeks ago,
trying to score an interview. He'd said he wanted a family member's perspective. She'd refused and then gone to

the sheriff to ask for protection. Again, they did nothing to stop the intrusion, saying no laws had been violated.

Even Charles Alcorn, the town's wealthiest resident, had reached out to her. He'd helped with the search years ago and said he'd like to offer assistance again. What could he do that hadn't already been done?

This time, the sheriff's office couldn't ignore her. They would have to do something. The attack was concrete and too close for comfort. The man had shown up out of nowhere. She'd been so focused on getting away that she hadn't thought to see if he'd retreated to a car. A make and model, a license plate, would give the sheriff something to go on.

Her best chance at seeing him behind bars, overdue justice for her brother, had just slipped away. *If* that was him, a little voice inside her head reminded.

Did he have her cell phone? A cold chill ran down her back.

Wait a minute. Couldn't the sheriff track him using GPS?

Anger balled inside her as she drove the couple of blocks to the sheriff's office. What if they didn't believe her?

She hadn't physically been there in years, and yet she could still recall the look of pity on Sheriff Randall Brine's face the last time she'd visited. His gaze had fixed on her for a couple seconds, contemplating her. Then, he'd said, "Have you thought about getting away for a little while? Maybe take a long vacation?"

"I'm fine," she'd said, but they both knew she was lying.

"I know," he'd said too quickly. "I was just thinking how nice it'd be to walk through the surf. Eat fresh

seafood for a change." Deep circles cradled his dark blue
eyes and he looked wrung out. She'd written it off as guilt,
thinking she was probably the last person he wanted to
see. Was she a reminder of his biggest failure? Then again,
it seemed no one wanted to see her around. "We've done
everything we can. I wish I had better news. I'll let you
know if we get any new information."

"But—"

His tired stare had pinned her before he picked up his
folder and refocused on what he'd been reading before
she'd interrupted him.

Rebecca had wanted to stomp her feet and make a
scene to force him to listen to her. In her heart, she knew
he was right. And she couldn't depend on the sheriff to
investigate every time something went bump in the night
or a complete stranger reminded her of him.

Somehow, life had to go on.

Heaven knew her parents, overwrought with grief, had
stopped talking to each other and to their friends. Instead
of real conversation, there'd been organized searches,
candlelight vigils and endless nights spent scouring fields.

When search teams thinned and then disappeared altogether, there'd been nothing left but despair. They'd
divorced a year following Shane's disappearance. Her
dad had eventually remarried and had two more children, both boys. And her mother never forgave him for
it. She'd limited visitation, saying she was afraid Rebecca
would feel awkward.

After, both parents had focused too much attention
on Rebecca, which had smothered her. There'd been two
and a half years of endless counseling and medication
until she'd finally stood up to them. No more, she'd said,
wanting to be normal again, to feel ordinary. And even

though she'd returned to a normal life after that, nothing was ever normal again.

Although the monster hadn't returned, he'd left panic, loneliness and the very real sense that nothing would ever be okay again.

Since then, she'd had a hard time letting anyone get close to her, especially men. The one person who'd pushed past her walls in high school, Brody, had scared her more than her past. He'd been there that night. He'd stepped forward and said she was meeting him to give him back a shirt he had to have for camp so she wouldn't have to betray her friends. Her mother had never forgiven him. He'd been the one person Rebecca could depend on, who hadn't treated her differently, and he deserved so much more than she could give. Even as a teenager she'd known Brody deserved more.

Separating herself from him in high school had been the right thing to do, she reminded herself. Because every time she'd closed her eyes at night, fear that the monster would return consumed her. Every dark room she'd stood in front of had made her heart pound painfully against her chest. Every strange sound had caused her pulse to race.

And time hadn't made it better.

She often wondered if things would have turned out differently if she'd broken the pact and told authorities the real reason they'd been out.

Probably not. She was just second-guessing herself again. None of the kids had been involved.

Once Shane had been discovered following her, they'd broken up the game and gone home. Nothing would've changed.

Rebecca refocused as she pulled into a parking spot at

the sheriff's office. By the time she walked up the steps to the glass doors, she'd regained some of her composure.

The deputy at the front desk acknowledged her with a nod. She didn't recognize him and figured that was good. He might not know her, either.

"How can I help you?"

"I need to speak to the sheriff."

"Sorry. He's not in. I'm Deputy Adams." The middle-aged man offered a handshake. "Can I help you?"

"I need to report an assault. I believe it could be connected to a case he worked a few years ago." She introduced herself as she shook his hand.

The way his forehead bunched after he pulled her up in the database made her figure he was assessing her mental state. Her name must've been flagged. He asked a few routine-sounding questions, punched the information into the keyboard and then folded his hands and smiled. A sympathetic look crossed his features. "I'll make sure the report is filed and on the sheriff's desk as soon as he arrives."

Deputy Adams might be well intentioned, but he wasn't exactly helpful. His response was similar as she reported her missing phone.

Not ready to accept defeat, she thanked him, squared her shoulders and headed into the hot summer sun.

Local law enforcement was no use, and she'd known that on some level. They'd let the man slip through their fingers all those years ago and hadn't found him since. What would be different now?

She thought about the fact that her little brother would be twenty-two years old now. That he'd be returning home from college this summer, probably fresh from an athletic scholarship. Even at seven, he'd been obsessed with sports. Maybe he still was. A part of her still refused to believe he was gone.

Rebecca let out a frustrated hiss. *I'm so sorry, Shane.*

What else could she do? She had to think. Wait a minute. What about her cell? If her attacker had picked it up, could she track him somehow? Her phone might be the key. She could go home and search the internet to find out how to locate it and possibly find him. And then do what? Confront him? Alone? Even in her desperate state she knew that would be a dangerous move.

Could she take Alcorn up on his offer to help?

And say what?

Would he believe her when the sheriff's office wouldn't?

She needed help. Someone she could trust.

Brody? He was back from the military.

Even though she hadn't seen him in years, he might help.

If she closed her eyes, she could remember his face perfectly. His honest, clear blue eyes and sandy-blond hair with dark streaks on a far-too-serious-for-his-age face punctuated a strong, squared jaw. By fifteen, he was already six foot one. She couldn't help but wonder how he'd look now that he was grown. The military had most likely filled out his muscles.

When she'd returned to school after a year of being homeschooled, kids she'd known all her life had diverted their gazes from her in the hallway when she walked past. Conversations turned to whispers. Teachers gave her extra time to complete assignments and spoke to her slowly, as if she couldn't hear all of a sudden. Even back then, the pain pierced through the numbness and hurt. She'd felt shunned. As the years passed, she realized no one knew what to say and she appreciated them for trying. She got used to being an outsider. Her tight-knit group of friends had split up. She'd figured they were afraid to be connected with her or just plain afraid of her.

Not Brody. He'd stopped by her house every day after the incident even though her mother refused to allow him inside, especially after he'd stepped forward. It had been easier to take the blame than to admit why they'd really been out that night—to play Mission Quest. They'd had good reasons to lie, too. First of all, they weren't supposed to be playing that online game, let alone sneaking out to meet up with strangers to capture their friends' bases. And then there was the sheriff. He'd been looking for any excuse to bust their best friend Ryan's older brother, Justin, the guy who'd let them into the game in the first place. If they didn't cover for him, the sheriff would go after Justin like an angry pit bull. It would be his third strike and a one-way trip to a real jail. No more acting-out-against-an-abusive-father juvenile stuff. He'd be shipped off for good if their dad didn't beat Justin to death first.

Justin had cleaned up his act. And he deserved a second chance. Besides, it was no surprise that he'd taken a wrong turn in the first place with a father as cruel as his. The real miracle had been that Ryan hadn't followed in his older brother's footsteps.

Even though it would have meant turning on their friends, Brody had visited Rebecca in the middle of the night to tell her that she didn't have to keep the pact. Ryan would understand.

But Justin didn't have anything to do with Shane's disappearance. And there was no reason to screw up another family.

Shaking off the memories, Rebecca slipped into the

driver's seat and started the engine. She put the car in Reverse and tapped the gas a little too hard.

An object flew forward underneath her feet. She hit the brake, bent forward and picked it up. Her cell. It must've fallen out when she was rushing into her car earlier.

A mix of relief and exasperation flooded her as the thought of tracking her assailant via her phone disintegrated.

It was too early to give up hope of finding him this time.

She couldn't do it alone. Brody had bought the old Wakefield Ranch. Rumor said he'd become a warrior overseas. Would he help? Could she reach out to him after all these years? How hard would it be to get his phone number and find out?

Rebecca pulled into another parking spot and thumbed through her contacts. Her finger hovered over Ryan's number. They hadn't spoken in years, but she figured it wouldn't hurt to reach out to him. She sent a text message to him, unsure this was his number anymore. It didn't matter. It was worth a try. He still owed her one for helping to protect his brother.

The text came thirty seconds later with Brody's information.

Seeing it, needing to reach out to him, made this horror so much more real. And her heart pitched when she thought about facing him again.

BRODY FIELDS LEANED against his truck. The call from Rebecca Hughes had dredged up old feelings best left buried. He'd almost ended the call without finding out what she'd wanted. Except he couldn't do that to her. It was

Rebecca. The sound of her voice had stirred up all kinds of memories. Most of them were good.

He'd known her since they were kids, but they'd been teenagers when he'd fallen for her. There was so much more than her physical beauty that had drawn him in. She'd been the only female Brody had ever trusted and allowed inside his armor after his mother had betrayed the family, stolen money from the town and then disappeared.

The mental connection he'd shared with Rebecca had been beyond any closeness he'd experienced. Looking back, maybe it was the loner in him that could relate to her isolation.

When she'd pushed him away and said she'd never loved him, it had hurt worse than any physical blow. Soon after, she'd left for college, and then eventually moved to Chicago. He'd been the most surprised to learn that she'd moved back to Mason Ridge.

For a split second, he'd hoped she'd called for old times' sake. Then, he remembered what day it was—the anniversary of Shane's disappearance—and he knew better.

The conversation had been short. She'd told him what had happened and requested to meet face-to-face at The Dirty Bean Coffee Shop. He'd agreed, ending their exchange. The place was on his way home. Driving to the meeting point had taken ten minutes.

The pale blue sedan parking next to his truck had to be hers.

Knowing she was about to step out of her car and he was about to see her again hit him hard. How many times had he secretly wished he'd run into her in the past few months? Where'd that come from?

Hearing that her abductor had returned hadn't done good things to Brody's blood pressure. He wouldn't refuse her plea for help. And a little piece of him hoped he'd figure out if her case and the memories were the reasons she'd rejected him all those years ago. He'd been a boy back then. Helpless. *A lot's changed.*

He'd grown up. Survived his mother's betrayal of his family and the town. Served his country. Gone on to become a leader of an elite-forces team. Spent time with a lot of interesting women. To be honest, not all of them were interesting, but they were smokin' hot.

He crossed his arms over his chest and tucked his hands under his armpits.

The first thing he noticed as Rebecca exited her vehicle was her jean-clad long legs and red boots. His body instantly reacted to seeing the woman she'd become. There were enough curves on her lean figure to make her look like a real woman. She still had the same chestnut-brown hair that fell well past her shoulders in waves. She'd be close enough for him to look into her light brown eyes soon. Were they still the color of honey?

Why did seeing Rebecca reduce him to being that heartsick seventeen-year-old brat again?

Brody ignored the squeeze in his chest. Fond memories aside, he didn't do that particular brand of emotion anymore.

That she moved cautiously, surveying the area, reminded him why she was there. It wasn't to talk about old feelings.

"It's good to see you." She took a tentative step closer to him.

Yep. Same beautiful eyes. Same diamond-shaped face. Brody hadn't expected her voice to sound this grown-up. Or so damn sexy. He didn't want to think about her in a sexual way. She'd been all sweetness and innocence to him at seventeen. And this wasn't a date. He glanced around the parking lot to make sure no one had followed her.

"Wish the circumstances were better. I'm glad you called." The conversation needed to stay on track. So, why did he feel another physical blow when he saw disappointment flash in her eyes? "Tell me why you think I can help."

"He's after me. Neither the sheriff nor the FBI caught him before. I'm scared. You're the only one I can talk to who knows what really happened that night." Her eyes flashed toward him nervously. "I've heard about the things you did overseas. I know you've done some security consulting on the side since you came back. I'd like to hire you to protect me while I sort all this out."

"I don't need your money. I'll help." He didn't have to think long about his answer. Brody had experience tracking down the enemy, and this case had always eaten at him. Guilt?

"I'd still like to pay you something. In fact, I'd rather do it that way. I'm not a charity case." She stared at him, all signs of vulnerability gone from her almond-shaped eyes.

He stared back. "Fine. We'll figure something out."

"Thank you."

He hadn't expected her to look so relieved. "You want to grab a cup of coffee while you fill me in?"

She nodded.

Brody followed Rebecca to the counter, where they placed their orders. She reached in her purse to pay for hers. He caught her arm. Big mistake. An electric volt shot through his hand, vibrated up his arm and warmed places that he didn't realize were still iced over.

There'd be no use denying he felt a sizzle of attraction being near Rebecca again. It was more than a mild spark. She'd grown into a beautiful woman. But if he didn't watch himself, she could put a knife through his chest with just a few words. And Brody had no intention of handing over that power again to anyone.

When their coffees were ready, she located a table in the corner. Brody followed, forcing his gaze away from her backside, ignoring how well the jeans fit her curves.

She took the opposite seat, her gaze diverting to someone behind him. Brody turned in time to see a fairly tall man sit a little too close for comfort. Then again, these coffee shops sure knew how to pack a hundred people into two-foot-square spaces. Brody had had to squeeze between the stacked tables to fit into the tight spot.

"Can you start right now?" Shoulders bunched, jaw set, she looked ready to jump if someone shouted an order over the hum of conversation. Tension practically radiated off her.

"Yes. I'll need to arrange care for my horses. I can make a call to cover that base. If I'm going to be able to help, you'll have to tell me everything." His voice was gruffer than he expected, borderline harsh. Between his need to be her comfort and inappropriate sexual thoughts, being near her wasn't exactly bringing out the best in him.

She glanced from side to side, told him what had happened that morning with more details this time, and then focused those honey browns on him. Tears welled in her eyes. "After all this time, he's after me, Brody. Why? It doesn't make any sense. Where's he been all these years?"

"That's a good question. One I intend to answer."

"And what about my brother? Is there any chance he could still be alive?" Her voice hitched on the last word.

"We'll find out." Brody gripped his cup so he wouldn't

reach out to comfort her. "You've already been to the sheriff or you wouldn't be calling me."

She lowered her gaze. "Yes."

"What did he say?" The way she kept one eye on the door had Brody thinking he needed to ask her to switch seats so he'd have a better view. As it was, he didn't like his back facing the door.

"That I should be careful and to call if I see or hear anything suspicious."

"Did you tell them that's why you were there in the first place?" Frustration ate at him. He needed to control it in order to focus on the mission. Why would the man who'd abducted her and her brother all those years ago come back? To finish the job with her? She'd never been the intended target. When she'd witnessed a man grab her brother and run, she'd chased him into the woods. He had to know she hadn't seen or remembered enough of him to help the law track him down or he'd already be in jail. "It's been fifteen years. Why now? Where's he been?"

"Wish I knew." Her gaze ping-ponged from the front door to the exit. Fear pulsed from her. "Then again, the papers always dredge up the past."

"That wouldn't suddenly bring him out. They run stories every year." Brody tapped his finger on the table. "I've thought about this a lot over the years."

"Did we do the right thing back then? I mean, we were just kids protecting our friend by keeping that secret. What if that cost Shane his... What if someone saw something?"

"They would've come forward on their own if they had. Unless you think Justin was somehow involved?"

"No. It wasn't him. This guy was too tall. Plus, I remember that smell. No one in Ryan's house smelled like apple tobacco, least of all Justin." The admission brought a frown to her lips.

"The sheriff wrote the case off as a transient passing through town before and found nothing. It's time to change things up. We need to look at this through a new lens. Our guy could be connected to Mason Ridge in some way. This is where it all started and this is where it ends." Brody had every intention of following through on that promise.

And if that meant breaking the pact and digging up the past, so be it.

Chapter Two

Rebecca's shoulders slumped forward. "It's no use. We've been over this a million times and we never get anywhere. I've scoured the internet for years trying to find Shane. The case is closed. It was most likely a random mugging this morning. Even the deputy thinks I'm crazy."

"Except that we both know you're not." Brody resisted the urge to take her hand in his, noticing how small hers was in comparison, how much more delicate her skin looked.

"The sheriff told me years ago the trail had gone cold. I just didn't want to accept the truth. They're probably right. Shane's...long gone." Her almond-shaped eyes held so much pain.

"I know why your parents didn't leave the area after they divorced. They never gave up hope of finding him, especially your mother," Brody said, leaning forward. Everyone in town had held out the same hope Shane would be found. Hope that had fizzled and died as the weeks ticked by. "And neither did you."

"Seemed like a good enough reason to stay in the beginning."

"There's no reason to give up now."

"Do you know how slim the chances of solving a cold

case are? I do." When she looked up, he saw more than hurt in her eyes. He saw fear. He already noted that she'd positioned herself in the corner with her back against the wall, insuring she could see all the possible entry points. And didn't that move take a page out of his own book?

"Except the case isn't cold anymore. He struck again. We know he's in the area."

"Do you have any idea how that new deputy looked at me when I reported the crime and he pulled me up in the system? No one believes me." Tears welled in her eyes, threatening to fall.

"I do." Brody meant those two words.

"He could be anywhere by now."

"And so could you. But you're not. You're here. And so is he." Brody needed the conversation to switch tracks. Give her a chance to settle down. It was understandable that her emotions were on a roller coaster. Her need to find her brother battled with the fear she never would. "What about after college? You disappeared. I heard that you swore you'd never set foot in Mason Ridge again. What happened?"

"I did. I moved to Chicago and got a job at a radio station. I came home three years ago because of my mom's health. She took a turn."

"I didn't know." Again he suppressed the urge to reach across the table and comfort Rebecca, dismissing it as an old habit that didn't want to die.

"I had no way to reach you while you were overseas. Doubt I could've found the right words, anyway."

Brody understood the sentiment. How many times had he thought about looking her up on social media over the years but hadn't? Dozens? Hundreds? "Is it her heart again?"

Rebecca nodded. The sadness in her eyes punctuated what had to be another difficult time for the Hughes family.

"What'd the doctor say?"

"That she isn't doing well. They're doing everything they can, but she's refusing to try a new medication that will help her. Says she's afraid of being allergic to it, which is just an excuse." She shrugged. "I always stop by and see her after I get groceries on Fridays. I couldn't go today, after what happened this morning. I called to let her know and prayed that she didn't pick up on anything in my voice. She shouldn't see me like this. It'll just make her worry even more."

"I'm truly sorry about your mom." And so many more things he wasn't quite ready to put into words. His own mother had freely walked away from his family after getting folks to hand over their hard-earned money under the guise of making an investment in Mason Ridge's future. She had no idea what it was like to stick around.

"Thank you." The earnestness in her expression ripped at his insides. "I can't help but feel that trying to reopen Shane's case is hopeless. The task force took all the facts into account fifteen years ago when they investigated his disappearance. All the leads from the case are freezing cold by now. My brother is still missing, probably dead. We're right where we started, except now this jerk's back as some twisted anniversary present to me." Tears streamed down her cheeks.

Brody reached across the table and thumbed them away, ignoring the sensations zinging through his hand from making contact with her skin and the warning bells sounding off inside his head.

She glanced at him and then cast her gaze intently on

the table, drawing circles with her index finger. "It's all my fault. If I hadn't told him to sit down and wait for me by the willow tree so I could finish the mission he'd still be alive today."

"Don't do that to yourself. None of this is your fault."

Her shoulders slumped forward. "What else can we do?"

Yeah, her stress indicator was the same. And Brody wanted to make it better.

"I'll figure out a way to get a copy of the file so I can review the list of suspects again. I have a friend in Records and she owes me a favor. Fresh eyes can be a big help and might give us more clues." Brody rubbed the stubble on his chin.

"With the festival going on this guy could blend in again, couldn't he?"

"Yeah. We have to look at everything differently this time. He might be someone local who hides behind the festival. Maybe he knew that was the first place law enforcement would look."

"You're right. He could be a normal person, a banker or store clerk." A spark lit behind her eyes, and under different circumstances it'd be sexy as hell.

"It's likely. He could be married and involved in a church or youth group. He might be a bus driver or substitute teacher. It's very well possible he could work with kids or in a job where he has access to families. We have to consider everyone. Those are great places to start."

"I just focused on what the sheriff had said before, him being transient. None of these options occurred to me." She shuddered.

Brody sipped his coffee. "It's not a bad thing that you don't think like a criminal."

"If we need help, Charles Alcorn offered," she said.

"A man in his position would be a good resource to have on our side." Brody leaned forward. "So this is how it's going to go. I follow you. Everywhere. You got a date, I'm right behind you." The thought of sitting outside her house while another man was inside doing God knows what with her sat in his stomach like bad steak. And yet, they were both grown adults. It shouldn't bother him. Wasn't as if he'd been chaste, either.

"I'm not dating."

Brody suppressed the flicker of happiness those words gave him. He had no right to care.

"And I don't want to stop you from doing…whatever," she added quickly.

Why did the way she said that knife him?

"Don't worry about my personal life. I'm here to do a job. That's all I care about right now." Why was that more of a reminder for him than for her?

Working with her was going to be more difficult than he'd originally thought. And not because errant sexual thoughts crossed his mind every time he got close enough to smell her shampoo. It was citrus and flowery. Being with her brought up their painful past, but they'd shared a lot of good memories, too. Like their first kiss. They'd skipped the Friday afternoon pep rally junior year and headed down to the lake in the old Mustang he'd bought and fixed up using money from his after-school job at his dad's garage.

As they sat on the hood of his car parked in front of Mason Ridge Lake, she'd leaned her head on his shoulder. And then decimated his defenses when she looked up at him with those honey browns. His heart had squeezed in the same way it did earlier today when he saw her again.

She still had that same citrus and flowery scent and it made his pulse race just as it had before. He remembered the warmth of her body against his side, her soft lips as they slightly parted.

Brody had leaned in slowly and her lips gently brushed against his; her tongue flickered across his mouth.

Afterward, they'd just sat there, silent, before he'd pulled her into a hug.

The kiss had lasted only a few seconds but was burned into his memory. How many times had he thought about those sweet lips when he was an ocean away with his face in the dirt? How many times since? *Too many*.

Brody glanced at his watch. "I'll connect with my friend and see what I can find out about that file."

"Okay." She leaned forward, rubbing her eyes, suppressing a yawn. "What else?"

"You used to look for Shane everywhere. My guess is that you haven't stopped. Am I right?"

"Yes. I scan social media on my days off."

"Any hits?"

She shrugged. "Not real ones. I've been hit on plenty, though."

"Men can be such jerks."

"Women are far worse. You'd be shocked at the messages I get from someone calling herself Adriana." Rebecca rolled her eyes.

"I have a few like those, too," he said in an attempt to lighten the tension.

"I'm sure you've been exposed to worse, having been in a war zone."

"I've seen my fair share of everything, here and abroad," he said. "You ever follow up on any of those real messages?"

"A handful. Why?" She paused and her eyes grew wide. "You don't think one of them could be stalking me?"

"Not sure. I was thinking it might be a good place to start."

She brought her hand up and squeezed the bottom of her neck on the left side, subconsciously trying to ease the tension in her shoulders. Her face muscles bunched. Signs her stress levels were climbing.

"Has anything else out of the ordinary happened to you recently? He had to know your schedule to know where you'd be this morning. I don't believe the grocery store was a random encounter."

"Now that you mention it, I've been hearing noises in the evenings before I leave for work. I thought it was the neighbor's cat at first. Now, I'm wondering if it could've been him."

"We'll check the perimeter of your house. The recent rain might have left us with evidence."

There'd been one of those open-up-the-sky-and-let-the-rain-pour-down-in-buckets storms North Texas was known for the other night. She scooted her chair back and slung her purse strap over her shoulder.

"There was also that unusually persistent reporter last week. I think his name is Peter Sheffield. I got off a few minutes early, so I was alone in the parking lot. He nearly gave me a heart attack waiting at my car after my shift at the radio station. Do you think he could be involved?"

"From here on out, I want you to suspect every sound, every person." Brody's gaze narrowed.

"So, what you're saying is…act like I always do."

He didn't like the sound of those words. "This guy might've been trying to scare you into an interview."

"That's crazy. People actually do that?"

Brody tapped his knuckles on the table. "I remember him now. He used to hang out with Justin, didn't he? Then he dropped out of Texas State U to join the military."

"That's right. He did. Are you saying you think he might be involved?"

"We need to look at everyone who was out that night playing the game. And especially Justin's friends."

Rebecca nearly choked on her sip of coffee. "I hadn't thought about it being someone so young. The apple tobacco. I just figured it had to be someone older."

"Maybe it is. But we're not taking anything for granted this time." He took the last swig of coffee, tilted the cup and glanced at the bottom, then fixed his gaze on her. "You ready to do this?"

She nodded, stood, walked past him and headed straight to the door.

"I'll follow you home in my truck." He threw away their empty cups, checking to make sure no one in the place seemed interested in either one of them. No one did.

Outside, the midday sun shone bright. Rebecca hesitated before spinning around to face him. He expected to be confronted with the same fear in her eyes, but she popped up on her tiptoes and brushed a kiss to his lips. "I'm not sure what I would do without you. Thank you, Brody."

The way his name rolled off her tongue brought back all kinds of memories he didn't need to be thinking about right now. "I haven't done anything yet."

"Yes, you have. An hour ago I was afraid of my own shadow."

"And now?"

"I'm relieved you're here. You look good, Brody."

The warmth her words spread through his chest almost

made him wonder if going to her place was a good idea. He was a grown man, now. And he had desires to match.

"You do, too. Better than good." Brody took her hand in his, ignoring how right it felt, and walked her to her vehicle.

Once she was safely inside, he hopped in his truck and followed Rebecca home. Her house, a two-bedroom bungalow, was fifteen minutes from the coffee shop. He parked behind her car as he surveyed the quiet residential street. Since the attack had happened hours ago, the monster could be anywhere. No red flags, yet.

"How long have you lived here?" he asked, once they'd both exited their vehicles, examining the front windows for any signs of forced entry.

"I rented it three years ago when I moved back." Her hand shook as she tried to unlock the door.

"I can do that for you." He looped his arm around her waist as she turned to face him. Touching Rebecca came a little too naturally, so he pulled back rather than allow himself to get sucked into the comfort.

"Guess I'm still a little shaken up." She smiled weakly as she handed over the key ring. Her fingers brushed against his flat palm, causing a sizzle to spread through his hand.

"You're doing great, honey." He closed his fist around the key, then stepped beside her before unlocking and opening the door. A high-pitched note held steady until she hit numbers on the keypad, four beeps followed by silence. The state-of-the-art security system was no surprise, given her past.

This place was all Rebecca. Soft, earthy feminine colors. Furniture he could see himself comfortable on—especially with her nearby. Her place was exactly as he'd imagined it would be, which had him thinking about the strong mental connection they'd shared. Still shared?

That was a long time ago. People change. He'd changed.

Walking around the living room, he ran his hand underneath lamp shades, tables and other flat surfaces.

The coffee-colored cabinets in the kitchen were his taste, too. He checked them and then swept his hand along the white marble countertops, stopping at the sink. There was a nice-sized window looking onto the backyard. The best thing about this part of North Texas was having trees. Her yard was a decent size, so someone could easily hide and watch her while she worked in the kitchen. Especially if she stood at the sink. His first thought was to install blinds.

Brody started making a mental to-do list as he moved through the house. He'd run to the nearest big-box store and pick up supplies later. He could make the changes himself.

She had a decent alarm.

"Do you live here by yourself?"

"Yeah." She bit back a yawn. Dark circles cradled her brown-as-honey eyes.

"You should try to rest. I'm not going anywhere. I'll wake you if I get any new information."

"I'm okay." She moved to the kitchen. "Besides, my nerves are too fried to sleep. I can't force down another cup of coffee. Want some herbal tea?"

"No, thanks." He still needed to check the master bedroom and he couldn't stall any longer. He shuffled his boots down the hall. The thought of being in the exact place she brought other men didn't sit well. There'd been no framed pictures of her with another guy so far. Brody didn't want to admit how happy that made him.

Hoping his luck would continue, he breached her bedroom. He'd open the nightstand drawer last, in case there were condoms. It wasn't his business what she did anymore, or with whom, but he couldn't help feeling territorial about his first love. The thought of her in bed with another man would rank right up there as one of his worst mental pictures. And he really didn't want to see any leftover men's clothing or shavers in the bathroom, either. Which was exactly the reason he'd put off checking her master bedroom.

As he walked the perimeter of the room, nothing stood out.

"Everything okay in here?" The sound of her voice coming from the doorway coupled with the visual of her bed didn't do good things to him.

"Doesn't look like you slept here last night."

"I work deep nights at the radio station."

"Right. Of course." Why did that ease his tense shoulders?

She stopped, almost as if she was hesitating to cross the threshold. Did she sense the heat filling the short distance between them? All he had to do was reach out and he could pull her close to him, protect her.

Brody mentally shook off the thought and moved on. "What time did you go to work last night?"

"I go in at ten o'clock. The show airs from midnight to six. We always wrap afterward."

"Any new employees in the last couple of months?"

"No. Not much ever really changes in this town." Her smile warmed his heart, threatening to put another crack in his carefully constructed armor. He took a couple of steps toward the door.

"The body needs sleep in order to perform. Why don't you close your eyes and rest while I check out the grounds?"

She looked up at him with big, fearful brown eyes. "You're not leaving, are you?"

"No. You're stuck with me. Like I said, I'm not going anywhere without you until we figure this whole thing out." He shouldn't notice how good he felt when her face muscles relaxed into a smile. "I need to make some calls, though, and you might as well get some shut-eye."

"What if he…" She didn't finish, but Brody knew exactly what she was going to say.

"I doubt he'll show up while I'm here. Think about it. This creep snatched little kids before and then surprised you this morning, which sounds like someone who's afraid of confrontation. I doubt he has the gall to try something with me around."

She nodded and her shoulders lowered.

"You have an extra key?"

"Sure." She disappeared down the hall, returning a moment later with a spare held out on the flat of her palm. She relayed her alarm code.

Taking it caused his finger to brush her creamy skin again. The frisson of heat produced by contact pulsed straight from his finger, to his arm and through his chest. In the back of his mind, he was still thinking about the feel of her lips against his at the coffee shop, the taste of coffee that lingered.

Physical contact was a bad idea. If he couldn't find and keep his objectivity in this case, the moral thing to do would be to help her find someone who could.

"You need me, just shout," he said, resigned. He needed to get in touch with the sheriff's office, too. See if Brine would offer information about the case.

"Okay." She paused. "Any chance you could stay inside until I get out of the shower?"

"I'll be in the living room," he said, hearing the huskiness in his own voice. The last thing he needed was the naked image of her in his thoughts.

He almost laughed out loud. They'd been together in high school. Not in the biblical sense, but they'd been a couple. Twelfth grade was a long time ago. Feelings changed. Their current attraction was most likely residual. She was beautiful. No doubt about that. And she was exactly the kind of woman he'd ask out if they'd met today and could forget about the past. But all the extra chemistry he felt had to be left over from before. That was the only reasonable explanation. Because Brody hadn't felt like this toward any woman since her. And he'd been in several relationships over the years. Yet, something had always stopped him from taking the next step. Marriage was a huge commitment, he'd reasoned. There'd been no need to rush into a big decision like that.

"I saw a laptop in the living room. Mind if I use it?" he asked.

"Not at all. Go right ahead," she said.

"What's the password?"

"Capital *N-V-M-B-R*. Then the number fifteen."

Brody turned without giving away his reaction. November fifteenth was his birthday.

REBECCA CHECKED THE CLOCK. She'd showered, hoping the warm water would relax her strung-too-tight muscles, before the tossing-and-turning routine began. She flipped onto her right side and placed a clean sock over her eyes to block out the light.

Rolling back to her left, she repositioned the sock.

No luck.

The sun was firmly set in the eastern sky. She'd closed her black-out curtains. This was normally the time she'd be asleep, but the way her mind was spinning no way could she rest. All she could think about was the possibility of Shane being alive. Even she knew the chances were slim. And yet, odds didn't matter in her heart, where she still held hope.

She'd need more than a piece of material to block out her thoughts. Time was the enemy. A killer was after her. Thoughts of being locked in that shed brought the terrifying sensation of her abduction back. And everything that had happened after…

When she'd returned, the town had been in chaos. Volunteers were assigned to a search team. Hundreds of people fanned out over the fields surrounding Mason Ridge Lake. Others opened car trunks and abandoned structures. People carried guns and set up neighborhood patrols. Even the wealthiest man, Mr. Alcorn, had thrown considerable resources into the effort.

Later, searchers joined hands as they walked in a line through the fields near Mason High School.

Two FBI agents had taken up residence in the Hughes's front room. A half dozen crop dusters and military planes had circled the sky, searching. The 4-H club had sent riders out on horseback.

Local law enforcement had encouraged people to keep their porch lights on at night and be ready to report any activity that might be suspicious. The Texas State Police had set up a half dozen roadblocks. Railroad cars, motel rooms and the bus station were searched—as was every house in the city.

Shane's comb had been shipped off to the FBI lab near

Washington for analysis. As had his favorite toys—trucks, LEGO and his handheld game system.

Rebecca had suddenly found herself under twenty-four-hour watch. Dr. Walsh, her pediatrician, had checked her for signs of sexual assault.

When a week of fruitless searching had passed, authorities had alerted residents to look out for scavengers, believing that Shane's body might have been tossed into a field or nearby farm. They'd been told to keep an eye out for large gatherings of buzzards and crows and were advised not to touch a body if one was found.

It wasn't long after that the FBI ran out of steam. Reporters had been a different story. They'd followed her parents for months, relentless.

Normally, Rebecca forced those thoughts out of her mind, unable to think about them. Having Brody in the next room brought way more comfort than it should. She told herself no one would care about her more than him, and that's why his presence gave her such a sense of well-being. Nothing about her current situation should cause her to let her guard down. The last time she'd gone against her better judgment, she'd ended up in a shed out in the woods. And her brother…

She couldn't even go there. Couldn't sleep, either. She tossed the covers and pushed off the mattress. She threw on a pair of shorts and a T-shirt, pulled her still-damp hair into a ponytail and met Brody in the living room.

He glanced up from the laptop, a look of determination creasing his forehead, and offered a quick smile. "Can't sleep?"

"No. This time of year is always…challenging. So, dealing with all this other stuff has my system out of whack." She threw her arms up, exasperated.

Brody studied her. His clear blue eyes seemed to see right through her. "I've said it before, but we will figure this out. I already reached out to Ryan and he's following up with the others, trying to see if we can figure out a good time for everyone to meet." He patted a spot on the sofa right next to him. He looked good. Damn good. He'd filled out his six-foot-two frame nicely. He was all muscle and strength and athletic grace. His blond hair was cut tight with curls at the collar. He wore a simple shirt and jeans.

Rebecca took a seat next to him, ignoring how her stomach free-fell the minute she got close. "Have you heard anything from your contact?"

"Yes. She emailed as much as she could. The suspect list is long." He had a pen and notepad out, scribbling notes as he flipped through a file on-screen. "I'd also like to take a look at your social-media account."

"Sure." She waited for him to click on the icon before giving him the password. "Nice pen."

He glanced at it and nodded. "A present from the old man."

"How is your father?"

"He's getting older, but he'd never admit it." Brody half smiled, still maintaining focus. "I've been thinking of moving him onto the ranch. Hate the thought of him being alone. But he's stubborn."

"Sounds like someone else I know." She laughed. "I doubt he'll give up his own place without a fight. He's a good man. I always liked him."

Brody nodded, but his expression turned serious again as he studied the screen.

"Find anything useful?"

"Hold on." He clicked through her chat messages,

studying the accompanying faces. He stopped at one, considered it for a long moment and then clicked on the image, which opened the guy's home page. "There's something about this one. Randy Harper."

"If Shane was still…alive, I'd imagine him to look just like this. I mean, he and I look related, don't we?" Her cell, on the coffee table, buzzed. She picked it up and checked the screen. It was her father. She hit Ignore and tucked it half under her leg.

Brody had seen who the caller was. She steadied herself for the inevitable questions about why she was refusing to take her father's calls. The cell vibrated under her leg, indicating he'd left a voice mail. She didn't want to get into it with Brody right now, didn't want to think about her father's new life while she still hunted down what had truly happened to his old one.

She glanced up, catching Brody's stare. He didn't immediately speak. Then he said, "The others resemble you, too, but there's something special about Randy."

"I had the same feeling."

"How long ago did you find him?" he asked.

"Six months or so."

"He doesn't live far."

"Nope. But he didn't respond to my message. I've been doubling my efforts with him and a few others lately."

"The city of Brighton is located two counties east of here. I used to know a girl who lived out there while we were in high school…." His voice trailed off at the end, as if he suddenly realized who he was talking to.

Sure, a twinge of jealousy nipped at her. More than that, if she was being totally honest. But she had no right to own the feeling. Shoving it aside, she smiled. It was weak, at best, but Brody took the peace offering, returning the gesture.

He scrolled down the page. "He hasn't posted anything in months. He either hasn't been online or he's abandoned his page altogether."

"We can rule him out as a phony, then. He can't be a crackpot trying to rattle me if he doesn't even realize I've tried to contact him. Plus, he's too old to be Shane. Look at the birthdate."

"You're probably right, but if it was him, then he might not really know when he was born. I've read about cases of abducted kids being told lies about when and where they were born to make it more difficult for them to dig around in the past."

"Wouldn't he need an actual birth certificate to enroll in school? My stepmother had to produce that, shot records, and a current electric bill for my half brothers," Rebecca said. She didn't want to feel the spark of hope that Shane might actually still be alive. She wanted her brother to be somewhere safe—had dreamed it, hoped it and prayed it. But she didn't want to create false expectations based on a social-media page.

"A birth certificate can be made. For a price. The rest would fall into place from there. Maybe we can find some of Randy's friends. Dig around a little in his background. Pay him a visit." Brody scribbled down a few names. "I don't want to invite them into your social network, so we'll have to reach out another way."

He scanned through photo after photo on the home pages of the people connected to Randy. A good fifteen minutes had passed when Brody made a satisfied grunt. "Look here. At this pic. And this one. Then, this one. See what's in the background?" He displayed the pictures in a larger window to view one at a time. Three friends had tagged Randy at a local restaurant called Mervin's Eats.

"When was the last picture posted?" Rebecca asked as another flicker of excitement fizzed through her.

"Three months ago." Brody glanced at the clock on the bottom right-hand corner of the screen. "Too early to go and check out the place now. Looks like we just figured out where we're eating tonight, though." He pulled up another screen, his fingers working the keyboard, and pulled up the address to Mervin's Eats in Bayville, Texas. He copied down the address in his notebook.

This was the first promising lead she'd had in fifteen years. It was hard to contain the enthusiasm swelling inside her. "For so many years, everyone's said he's gone. What if they were wrong?"

"I have plans to track down every possibility. That means we're going to run into dead ends." His honest blue eyes had darkened with concern.

"Believe me, I know better than anyone about disappointment." He was trying not to get her hopes up in case he had to dash them, and she appreciated him for it. "I've handled it before and I will again. It just feels nice to have a little hope for a change."

His nod and smile said he understood. "We need to keep working other trails, too. If we can figure out why or how our guy was connected to Mason Ridge before, maybe we can figure out what he's doing here now."

"I can't stand waiting around. I'd like to go out looking for him."

"Okay. Give me a chance to study these notes so I have a better idea where to start searching. See if I can find some connection either to this town or to your family."

She shivered as an icy chill ran down her back. That

thought was unnerving. Could someone close to them have orchestrated Shane's disappearance? She hadn't considered it before.

Brody's gaze trained on her. "Have you eaten anything today?"

"Not yet. Stomach's been churning all morning. My brain, too. I was thinking about the fact the places where he took my brother and me weren't secure. It couldn't have taken him more than a half hour to get us both there, so they were close by. He had to know the area, which, now that I think about it, would rule out a random person passing through town. I told the sheriff all this before, but there's another thing I can't stop thinking about. He didn't want me. He wanted my brother. I got in the way when I followed them and the guy was distressed about it."

"Makes me think it might've been his first time to kidnap someone," Brody said quietly.

"Not the work of someone used to slipping into a strange town to snatch a kid."

"What else did the sheriff say?" Brody asked, his interest piqued.

"That he probably improvised, saw a couple of abandoned buildings and hid us there. But why? Wouldn't he want to get out of town as quickly as possible?"

"And the response to that?"

"Nothing to me. I did hear someone from the FBI tell my parents later that the guy most likely hadn't preplanned the kidnapping."

If she could go back and trade places with her brother, she wouldn't hesitate. How many times had she wished she'd been the one to disappear, to die?

There was a slim chance that Shane was still alive, she reminded herself. The odds weren't good, Rebecca knew that, but she also knew better than to focus her energy on the negative.

That bastard had made a mistake once. She was living proof. All she needed was another misstep. With Brody's eyes on this case, maybe he would figure it out and bring the monster to justice. Rebecca would do whatever it took to help. "If only I remembered more…"

Brody's arm around her shoulder, his fingers lifting her chin, stemmed the emotion threatening to unravel her.

"I hate that you're going through this again. I'm sorry it happened to you in the first place. Believe me, I'll do everything I can to find that jerk."

A mix of emotion played inside her. Fear. Anxiety. Sadness.

Hope?

"Let's get something to eat and we'll hit Woodrain Park. He's probably smart enough to pick a new place, but we have to cover it, anyway." His words wrapped around her like a warm blanket. She leaned over until their foreheads touched.

"I won't let him hurt you again." He said other sweet words—words that made her want to yield to his strength.

And yet, getting too close to Brody wasn't a good idea. No one could quiet the monster's voice in the back of her head for long. He would return. He always returned. And she'd slip into her armor, blocking out the world.

"I'll fix something to eat." She rose and walked toward the kitchen, stopping in front of the sink.

Brody followed. The gun tucked into the waistband of his jeans was a stark reminder of the dangers they faced. He rummaged around the fridge, tossing up an apple. "Not much here to work with."

"I left my groceries scattered across the lot."

He nodded and then searched the pantry, pulling out almond butter, bread and cinnamon grahams. "These'll work."

She nodded.

He moved to the sink with the supplies, glanced up and froze. His gaze fixed on something out the window.

Cursing, he palmed his weapon and adjusted his position, stepping away from the window. "Get down. Now."

Rebecca dropped to her knees as panic roared through her, making her limbs feel heavy. "What is it? What's going on?"

"Someone's out there watching."

Brody crawled past her with the agility and speed of a lion zeroed in on his prey. "Lock the door behind me. Wait right here until I get back."

"No," she pleaded, trying to stop her body from shaking. She opened the drawer and gripped a knife.

"Take me with you. I don't want to be here alone."

Chapter Three

"Stay close." Brody didn't like the cold chill pricking the hair on his arms. He didn't like how easily a stranger could watch Rebecca while she was in the house. And he sure as hell didn't like the fact that the man who'd tormented her and changed her life forever was most likely back.

Brody crouched low as he cleared the back door.

The figure, tall and thick-built enough to be a man, darted into the trees.

"Go inside, lock the door and set the alarm."

She didn't respond, but he heard her backtrack as he broke into a full run. No way could she keep up, and he didn't want to risk them being separated in the trees, leaving her exposed and vulnerable.

The unforgiving dirt and shrub stabbed his feet as he bolted across the yard. Brody regretted kicking his boots off and getting too comfortable. The male form disappeared to the left as Brody hopped the chain-link fence and breached the tree line.

Forging through the mesquites, maples and oaks, Brody winced as he stepped on scattered broken limbs. He pushed the pain out of his mind, maintaining full focus on his target. He could hear crunching ahead of him, although he couldn't judge the distance or the gap between them. At this point, the noise could come from an animal he'd spooked. Based on the weight, it would have to be one big animal. Even so, it was still possible. There was no telling for sure until he got eyes on whatever it was.

A dark thought hit. Brody was being drawn deeper into the trees; the underbrush was thickening, and Rebecca was alone at the house. Brody couldn't take the chance he'd been lured away.

Besides, the rustle of leaves was growing more distant, indicating the guy was too far ahead to catch.

Circling back, the pain of bare feet pounding against hard soil made running a challenge.

He didn't know how long he'd been going, but it took a good fifteen minutes to jog back to the bungalow. His feet had been cut and he was leaving a trickle of blood across the lawn on Rebecca's quarter-acre lot.

She must've been glued to the kitchen window, because as soon as he stepped onto the back porch, the door swung open and she rushed into his arms.

"Hey, hey." He took a step back as the full force of her impact hit him.

"I'm sorry." She buried her face in his chest.

Brody should put a little space between them. He should take a step back and not be her comfort. He should keep a safe distance.

Should.

But couldn't.

Not with the way she felt in his arms. Not with the way her body molded to fit his. Not with her scent, citrus and flowery, filling his senses.

A tree branch crunched. Brody scanned the yard, didn't see anything.

Outside, they were exposed.

He guided them inside the house, then closed and locked the door behind them.

"It's okay," he soothed.

"I know," she said quickly, and he knew it was wishful thinking on her part.

He heard her muffled sniffles and suspected she wasn't stepping away from him because she didn't want him to see her cry.

Before he could debate the sanity of his actions, his arms encircled her waist, hauling her closer to him.

Flush against his chest, he could feel her rapid heartbeat. The whole scenario might be erotic if she wasn't shaking so damn hard.

"SHOULD WE CALL the sheriff?" Maybe they'd believe her this time with Brody there to corroborate her story. Rebecca took a step away from him, and then stared out the window.

"And say what? I saw a guy in the tree line? He didn't break any laws being out there," Brody said, a frustrated edge to his tone.

"He knows where I live. God only knows how long he's been out there spying on me." A chill raced down her spine at the thought of him watching her through her windows. She wasn't safe even in daylight now.

Brody took a step toward her and put his hand on her shoulder.

She turned to face him, ignoring the shivers his touch brought. Determination set his jaw, and the cloud forming behind his eyes said he wasn't sure she would like what he had to say.

"I don't know if I can protect you here. We most likely

scared him off and he may not return, but it's a risk I'm not willing to take with you."

Those words sent an entirely different shiver down her body, a cold, icy blast that said everything she knew was about to be taken away from her again.

"Meaning what?"

"I need to take you someplace safe."

This bungalow might not be much, but it was her home. The thought of allowing that twisted jerk to force her out of her house churned in her stomach. He'd taken away so much already—from her, from her family. Part of her wanted to dig in her heels and argue because anything else felt as if she was sacrificing her power all over again. Except the logical part of her brain overrode emotion.

Brody had military experience. She'd hired him to keep her safe. Not listening to his advice would be more than stupid—it could be deadly.

His gaze stayed trained on her as she mentally debated her options. Options? What a joke that was.

So, she wouldn't be stupid. Of course, she'd go where she could be safe.

"I'll do whatever you need me to." The words tasted sour. Putting herself in Brody's hands wasn't the issue.

Relief relaxed the taut muscles in his face. "Good. Then, pack a bag and let's get out of here."

"Can we search for him? Go after him for a change? Maybe even put him on the run?"

"If that's what you want." His blue eyes darkened, the storm rising.

"I know what you're thinking. Yes, looking for him could be dangerous. I understand that and I need you to know I'm scared. But I'm also determined. He doesn't get to take away my power again. Sitting around, waiting for him to strike makes me feel helpless."

"I'll have your back. He has to get through me to touch you. And, darlin', that isn't happening on my watch."

Rebecca had sensed as much when they'd dated in high school. She'd gotten so used to being alone, to the isolation that came with being "damaged" and different. She'd quickly figured out where the term *kid gloves* came from. The sentiment might've been wrapped in compassion, but that didn't change the message to a child.

Well, she was no longer a child. And that psychopath didn't get to make her afraid anymore. Sure, she'd had a moment before in the kitchen. There'd be more, too. And she refused to apologize for her moments of weakness.

Being afraid was a good thing. It would make her cautious. It would keep her from making a stupid mistake that he could capitalize on. It would drive her to find him and possibly her brother, if Shane was still alive. Besides, being fearless had put her in this situation. She'd had no business sneaking out that night. Mason Ridge might've been the Texas equivalent of Mayberry, but complacency meant being vulnerable.

"I just need a minute." She moved to the bedroom and opened a suitcase, thinking about the few items she couldn't live without. A sad note played in her heart. She had a few articles of clothing that had a special meaning, but that was about it. Shane's Spider-Man watch, his favorite possession on the earth, was inside her drawer. She retrieved it and pressed it to her chest.

She missed him.

Still missed him.

Everything good about childhood disappeared that hot night in late June. It was as though her mother and father had died along with the memory of Shane. Rebecca had no recollections of spring-break trips or campouts. Her parents had become obsessed with keeping her alive and in sight. Sleepovers stopped. There were no more séances or s'mores over a campfire, like there had been when Shane was alive.

It was as though all the color had been stripped out of life. No more blue skies or green grass. No more laughter. She'd been so distraught with grief at the time she didn't notice that while other kids gathered outside at the park for ball, she'd engaged in therapy with one of her many doctors.

She'd existed, had been treated like fine china, put on a display shelf and only handled with the utmost care. She'd spent most of her time in her room because being downstairs with her parents while they fought that first year had been even more depressing. Books had given her an escape and kept her somewhat sane, somewhat connected to the world playing out in front of her, all around her and, yet, so far out of reach.

When her parents had divorced, the rest of her fragile world shattered.

The truth was that Rebecca couldn't connect with anyone after losing Shane. Deep down, she didn't blame her father for wanting to start a new life. He'd tried to include her, make her feel part of his new world. But that would've been a slap in the face to her mother. And Rebecca already felt as though her mother had suffered enough.

She placed the watch gently inside her bag, then opened the next drawer and pulled out a few pairs of jeans, undergarments, and a variety of shirts, shoving them inside.

Rebecca stomped to her closet and jerked a few sundresses off their hangers. After rolling them up, she stuffed them inside the bag, fighting the emotions threatening to overwhelm her.

Toiletries from the bathroom were next on her mental checklist. She moved into the en suite and grabbed her makeup bag.

A wave of nausea rolled through her. His voice. The apple-tobacco smell. Her brain had blocked everything else out. She couldn't remember what he looked like other than a nebulous description.

Not even her psychiatrist had been able to hypnotize that out of her. She wished like hell she would've been able to give the sheriff and the FBI more to go on. She was the only one who'd had a glimpse of him, the one who'd lived, and she couldn't pick him out of a lineup if her life depended on it.

And, now, it would seem that it did.

Rebecca didn't realize she was shaking, until Brody's steady arms wrapped around her, stabilizing her. "I was just thinking that I could've stopped all this if I'd just remembered."

"It's not your fault." His warm breath rippled down the back of her neck.

"I know, but—"

"It's not your fault."

Hadn't she heard those four words strung together a thousand times via counselors, teachers, her parents? "It just feels like if I'd been able to describe him—"

"Honey, there were grown men trained to track predators like him who couldn't get the job done. Him getting away wasn't the fault of a twelve-year-old girl."

On some level, she knew Brody was right. And, yet, guilt fisted her heart, anyway. He was being kind, so she'd spare him her true feelings. She tucked them away and forced a smile, ducking out of his hold.

"Good point." She moved to the bed, closed the suit-case and zipped it. "I've been thinking a lot about the old group. Think Ryan got ahold of them? All of us were out there that night. Maybe someone saw something they didn't realize could be important."

"I've been thinking the same thing. Ryan's working on getting everyone together. Dawson's not far. Dylan moved a town over, so he won't be hard to track down. We'll have to ask around for James. I don't know what happened to him after I left for the military. What about the girls? You talk to any of them?"

"Other than exchanging Christmas cards with Lisa and Samantha? No. Janet still lives here but I can't remember the last time we spoke and I don't think she was out that night. Melanie moved to Houston and never comes back."

"At least you have a few addresses. That's more than I have to go on. Maybe the others will know once we get the ball rolling." He paused. "I don't remember seeing Melanie that night, either, or James for that matter but we should try to reach them, anyway."

Brody walked over and gripped the handle to her suit-case. "I can take you home with me, or we can go to a hotel. The choice is yours."

"We should be good at a hotel." A neutral place might keep her thoughts away from how much Brody had grown into a man she could respect. She led the way through the house, stopping in the living room to grab her laptop. "Not sure when I'll be back, so I better take this."

"I'm going to want to dig deeper into a few of the re-sponses you received to your social-media messages."

"I almost forgot about the letters."

"You still have those?" Anger flashed in his blue eyes.

"Turned most over to the sheriff, but some new ones have turned up recently." She moved to the laundry room, where she'd been keeping the stack of mail.

More anger flashed in Brody's expression as she handed them over.

"There must be fifty letters here."

"This time of year always brings out the crazy in people." Arming the alarm, Rebecca had the feeling that once she walked outside she'd never be the same.

She locked the door behind them, hoping she could remember something else about that day…anything that might make the nightmare stop.

Chapter Four

Brody shouldn't want to show Rebecca his ranch, shouldn't want her to be proud of him. Hell, he'd already had her in his arms twice and he couldn't deny just how much it felt as if she belonged there, especially with the way her warm body molded to his. She'd asked to go to a hotel instead and his chest had deflated a little. The facts still remained the same. She'd rejected him and stomped on his heart before and she'd do it again. She wasn't cruel, just scared and confused. And it was all too easy for Brody to slip into his old role of being her shoulder to cry on, her friend. She'd confused those feelings for something else when they were young and she was doing it now. That was the only reason she'd go down that path again. How stupid was he not to figure it out before? Then again, Rebecca Hughes was his kryptonite. He reminded himself of the real reason she was there in the first place. She'd asked for his help.

All he was doing was helping Rebecca get her life back. He owed her that.

Or maybe he owed it to himself. If he got her squared away, he could put the past behind him and move on. He could stop thinking about those hauntingly beautiful eyes, the fear he saw behind them, the frustration he felt when he couldn't take it away.

"Got a different idea of where we can hang out the next few days instead of a hotel."

"Oh, yeah. Where are we headed?"

"How do you feel about camping?" He stole a glance at her as he pulled out of the drive, needing to see the look on her face. She might've been born in the country, but Rebecca Hughes didn't sleep outside.

Based on the look she shot him, his attempt at humor had only made things worse.

"Is that your idea of a joke?" She tapped his arm.

"Yes. It is." Something needed to break the tension. Get the conversation on a lighter track. It looked as if her muscles were strung so tight she might snap.

"Well, it's not funny." Her face screwed up. And she finally smiled, too.

"Sorry about the joke. But your reaction made me laugh. And I needed that."

"Okay, funny man. Where are we really going?" There was something special about the curve to her lips, the way her eyes flashed toward him looking so alive. The few times he'd broken through to her in high school were some of his happiest moments. And how sad did that make him sound? Then again, after his mother had ripped off the town and disappeared, life had become dark and complicated for him and his father.

"How do you feel about a serious change in plans? Hanging out in a cabin in Texoma for a few days until we sort all this out instead of a hotel? No roughing it. The place will have all the modern luxuries."

She was shaking her head from the second she heard "Texoma."

"It's too far. By the time we drive out there and back,

we'll lose four hours. No way." Her body had started shaking again, all hint of playfulness gone from her expression. He wondered if she even realized she was doing it.

"You sure you don't want to get away? I mean *really* get away?"

"I can't. I don't want to be that far from my mother. I need to call work, too. In fact, I should do that right now." She made a quick call and then dropped her phone in her purse. "I could always stay with my mother."

"That's not a good idea. Unless you want to tell her what's going on."

"No. You're right. It's bad enough that I skipped our visit this morning. That won't work. I'd rather keep her out of this as much as possible."

"I figured that's what you'd say."

"She needs me here. Can we get another place? Something closer?"

Brody stopped at the four-way stop sign at the end of her block. "My ranch is the perfect place."

"You bought the old Wakefield place, didn't you?"

"It's less than twenty minutes from here and it'll make it easier for me to check on the horses. If you really don't want to go there, my dad's house is another option."

"It would be nice to see him again. I'd like to stay at your place, though, if we can't stay at a hotel."

"It might be best if we don't leave a credit-card trail." He turned the steering wheel right. Pride he had no right to feel tugged at his heart. He needed to remember to keep a safe distance from the emotion. Nothing good could happen from touching a fire twice. "Let's swing by and get you settled before heading out to search for this guy."

"That's a better plan."

"Can I ask a question, though?"

"Okay." Her tone was tentative.

"Why didn't you take your father's call earlier? You two still at odds?"

"I'm not sure 'at odds' is the best way to describe our relationship. We don't really have one."

"Why is that, if you don't mind me asking?"

"It's complicated."

"I know." He kept his gaze on the road ahead. "I realize why you kept your distance before…how screwed up your mom was. I'm sure you felt conflicted. Love him and it betrays her. I get it. But, why now? Your mom's sick. You're doing all this alone and you don't have to."

"She's not his problem anymore."

"He said that?"

"No. Not in so many words. But he walked out. Divorced us."

"Her. He divorced *her*. There's a big difference."

"Same thing."

"Is it?" He shrugged. "I see Dylan with Maribel and just because he's not together with her mom doesn't mean he loves that little girl any less."

"Dylan has a daughter?" She couldn't contain her shock.

"Long story, but yeah. He's a great dad, too."

"He's the last person I'd expect to have a family. Especially after what happened to him with his own parents. Didn't we vote him most likely to become a career criminal?"

"What can I say? The guy cleaned up his act. He'd do anything for Maribel. He's a changed man."

Brody's phone vibrated again, another text. "Can you check that for me?"

Rebecca picked it up from the seat and checked the screen, staring for a long moment.

"It's from Ryan. He spoke to Lisa and she said one of her cousins was in Woodrain Park when a strange-looking guy ran past. He fit the basic description of our guy." Her voice cracked on the last few words.

Brody gripped the steering wheel so tight his knuckles went white. He ground his back teeth. "Looks like we have a place to start our search."

"SOMETHING'S BEEN BOTHERING me about this whole scenario." Brody finally broke the silence. "You asked the question before and it's the same one that's been on my mind. Why now? What's so significant about today?"

"I keep racking my brain, too. I always go back to the fact that it's the fifteenth anniversary."

"Yeah, but what's so important about this one? Why not the fifth, or the tenth?"

Good question. "Could it be the extra newspaper coverage we're getting this year?"

"It's possible. They run stories every year, right?"

"Uh-huh."

"Makes me think there was some kind of trigger that we haven't figured out yet."

"That makes sense. But what? I haven't done anything differently. I've been here working, taking care of my mother. My routine hasn't changed." Her life sounded depressing when she spoke about it out loud. It was true, though. Her entire world had been about existing and nothing more for more years than she could remember. Maybe didn't want to, either.

"You moved back a few years ago, so that's not it." He tapped the steering wheel with his thumb. "Any new friends?"

"I don't have time." She glanced down at her feet

when she said it. Was that true? Or had she simply not made time?

"What about those letters? Anything stand out?"

"No. I get the same stuff every year," she said on a sigh.

"Any new employees at work?"

"We have a summer intern who started last month."

"Male or female?" His tone deepened a fraction, but she noticed it. He was onto something.

"Male. What are you getting at?"

"Who is it?" Brody's gaze stayed fixed on the road ahead.

"Alex Sweeny. Why?"

"How tall is he?"

"Six feet, I guess." Surely Brody wasn't saying what she thought. That Alex was somehow involved. She was already shaking her head. "He's way too young to be the guy we're looking for. Plus, he's related to the sheriff."

"You're right. We have to explore every possibility, though. And one of those prospects is that this guy could be involved somehow or wanting you to relive the past." His jaw clenched and released. His tension level matched hers.

"You mean like a copycat?" Rebecca didn't want to consider the possibility. If this was some twisted person trying to remind her of that horrible summer, then her chances of figuring out what had happened to her brother were nil.

And if not?

Then she had to face the horrible truth that any whack job could send her spiraling back to that dark place by imitating the crime. "What about the apple tobacco? The officers and FBI were careful about not letting that leak into the press exactly for this reason. How would he know about that?"

Rebecca kept on alert for two things. One was the scent of apple tobacco. The other was Shane's birthmark. He had a birthmark that looked like Oklahoma on top of his right foot.

Brody's face set with concentration for a long period. "With Sweeny being related to the sheriff he could get inside information of your case."

"I hadn't even thought of that. He would know about the threatening letters. The reporter. It was all common knowledge around the radio station."

"Why?"

"My boss wanted everyone on the lookout. He figured the best way to protect me and keep his other employees safe was to keep everyone informed." But could Sweeny, a young kid, pull off an attack at the grocery store without her realizing who he was? "I still think the kid is innocent."

"And he might be. But until we figure this thing out, we follow through on every possible lead." Brody turned into Woodrain Park's lot.

Rebecca hadn't been back to that place, to those woods…ever. Icy chills raced up her arms. She crossed them to stave off goose bumps.

As if a door had been opened, emotions flooded, crashing into her.

The shed.

The desperation.

She stopped for a moment to stem the tears pouring down her cheeks. "I can't remember much of what happened in the shed. I must've blocked it out or something."

Brody had pulled over and parked. His hand covered

hers, which did little to stop the shaking. "He can't hurt you anymore."

"What if I can't do it? Can't go back in there?" She motioned toward the wooded path.

"Then we'll look somewhere else. The chance he'd return is slim."

His words, his touch, breathed life into her. And a bit of courage. Besides, she couldn't avoid those woods forever. Maybe going, facing that horrible place, might help her remember something else. "You're right. He's most likely long gone by now. And even if he's not I have to do this. It might help. I keep thinking about how my brother's disappearance is my fault." A sob racked her. "I wish he would've stayed home that night instead of sneaking out to follow me. Wish I hadn't gone out that night and then none of this would've happened."

"I remember how close you two were. How you stood up for him when that bully threatened to beat Shane up after school."

"And you showed up at the rock quarry to make sure the bully never pulled that on younger kids again," she said.

Brody shrugged.

"Sorry about the black eye he gave you."

"That healed. I'm not so sure my pride ever recovered," he said with a smile that could melt Glacier Bay.

She leaned into him, into his comfort. She rarely ever spoke about the past, let alone laughed at some of the memories. Being with Brody was slowly bringing her back to life. He seemed to understand her need to keep everyone at a safe distance. He did the same. Maybe it was that she knew he'd been a loner most of his life and she could relate—she'd felt the same every day since that summer night when her life inexplicably changed. The only happy thought she'd held on to through college was Brody. He'd been her safe landing.

Regret filled her as he sat there quietly reassuring her, and for a split second she wished she could go back and make things right. Would she have pushed him away if she'd known no other man's touch would make her feel the way his did?

"You don't have to do this." Brody's voice, warm and understanding, pulled her back to the present. "We can go. Let the others look here. Ryan's on his way as we speak and he's bringing Dylan."

"I want to." How did she explain that while she realized facing these woods, that shed again, would be the most difficult thing in her life, it was also the only way to begin healing? All these years, she'd been going through the motions of her day, numb. Being with Brody, remembering that it was possible to feel things again, made her want to keep going. Do more than just exist.

"I don't want to go, believe me. Everything inside me is telling me to run the other way. But I'm afraid I'll feel even worse if I don't. What if I could have saved him and didn't because I was scared to go back? I can't live with that."

"I understand." And the hitch in his voice said he meant those words. He got out of the truck and then opened the passenger door. "It's not still there, you know. The shed."

"What happened?"

He rolled his shoulders in a shrug. "Me."

"You came out here?"

"It was after you left for college. I'd signed up for the service. Didn't want to ship out with unfinished business here."

She understood he wouldn't see another answer to his emotions. Brody had been quick to anger before and ready to fight the world. Except when it came to her and his family. He'd been tender and kind, which had made pushing him away all that much more painful.

The military looked to have done good things for him. He seemed to have grown into his own skin, was more at peace with himself and the world. Except when it came to her. There, he seemed as confused as she felt.

"I couldn't stand this place for what it had done to you. The fact that it was still standing six years later made me furious. I had to make sure another soul would never be taken to that place again. So, I tore it apart with my own hands to make sure."

"Thank you." She could totally see Brody doing something like that to protect her, to protect others. Maybe even out of frustration that the guy got away with it. His angry streak never would have been aimed at her or any other innocent person. But a bad guy, someone who was downright mean to others, should watch out.

She'd noticed it before, but there was a sense of purpose to Brody's stride now. Less anger, more determination. He was quiet calm, but, just like the surface of the ocean, danger lurked below. She had no doubt that if Brody met the man who'd hurt her today, he'd unleash hell. Just like he'd done all those years ago when faced with a bully. This time, Brody would win.

He took her hand as he guided her toward the pathway in the woods.

His cell buzzed. He checked the screen. "It's Dylan."

"Let's hope for good news."

Brody tipped his chin. "Tell me you found something we can work with."

He said "uh-huh" a few times into the phone, but Rebecca could tell from his tone there was nothing new to go on.

"We're at the park. We just got here." He went quiet. "Then you're not far from us." Another pause. "Yeah. That's exactly where we're headed. I know, man. I hear you."

She knew immediately that they were surprised she'd want to go back there. She couldn't say she was shocked at their reactions. No one in her right mind would do it. Maybe if she followed the killer's trail, she'd find something. It was a long shot but she had to try for Shane. She'd been a kid before, helpless, but she wasn't anymore.

She'd thought about this a million times. If she'd screamed for help instead of following and confronting the kidnapper, would things have turned out differently? Or what if she'd left some sort of trail so that others could find them?

A knot formed in her chest, tightening like a coil with each forward step.

It wasn't hard to tune out the rest of Brody's conversation. Rebecca was half-afraid of what Dylan thought about her after the way she'd left things with Brody, and she was afraid she'd overhear him warning Brody to stay away from her or something.

The only thing keeping her feet moving at this point was Brody's hand on her lower back, guiding each forward step, reassuring her.

"Dylan and Ryan are near Mason Ridge Lake. Said they'd head this way."

She needed to focus her attention on something besides the horror inside her escalating the farther they walked. "How are they?"

"Dylan and Ryan? They're good. I already told you about Dylan's little girl."

"You said he was bringing her up alone. What happened?" She needed to distract herself. Her pulse was rising and she needed to think about something else besides what lay ahead.

"He met someone on leave and fell pretty hard. Guess he was missing home and she reminded him of it. The relationship didn't last long, which is a long story, but he got Maribel out of it."

"What about the mother?"

"She was really sick when she finally told Dylan he had a child. He got to see her one last time before…"

"That's so sad. He didn't know?"

"No. She didn't tell him. Said she was afraid of what his reaction would be."

"He always said parenting was the cruelest thing people could do to children. She must've known."

"He didn't keep his feelings a secret. You should see him now. Maribel came to live with him when she was two. He had a rough year adjusting, but you wouldn't know it to see them together now."

It was hard to think of Dylan being tender with a toddler. If Brody had been tough back in the day, then Dylan had been an outlaw. Throw them both together and they'd be deadly.

Seeing Brody now, thinking about children, made Rebecca wish she'd handled things differently. The deepseated sense of trust they'd shared was gone. She could see unease in his eyes. He was still as protective as he'd always been—some things would never change.

There were new scars on his body that weren't there before. He might've filled out in good ways, all muscle and strength, but he'd been hurt, too. Her heart squeezed thinking about the pain he must've endured. Rebecca knew full well external scars hurt far less than internal ones.

She'd lied to him and pushed him away. The only other time she'd been untruthful was for their friends.

Small towns were known for being bad places to hide secrets. Yet, they'd had to protect their friends. A cold chill raced up her spine, gripping her heart. A mistake?

The uneasy feeling intensified. Her feet felt heavier, legs weaker. A ball tightened in her chest.

Brody stopped. "You sure you want to keep going? You've been too quiet, which used to mean you were over-thinking something. Now, I have no idea if it still means that. But I can tell that whatever's going on is spiking your blood pressure."

A branch snapped.

She turned around and gasped. "Oh. God. No!"

Brody instinctively reacted, dropping down low and pulling her down with him, a second too late to miss the large metal object from cracking his skull.

Chapter Five

Brody fought against the darkness trying to invade his body. The blunt-force blow to his head scrambled his brains. He instinctively felt around for a knot. Didn't take long to find one the size of an egg.

There was blood on his hand when he brought it back down. Lots of blood. He felt around in his pocket for his cell. It must've fallen out when the blow knocked him off balance.

Dizzy, vision blurred, he scrambled to stop a tall man from dragging Rebecca into the thicket. She fought like a wildcat, kicking and screaming, but she was outmatched in height, weight and strength.

Brody grabbed dirt, stumps, anything that would help him gain purchase as he crawled on his belly toward the attacker. He reached out in time to catch the guy's ankle and latched on to his pants.

The last thing he remembered was being dragged several feet before the darkness clawing at him won.

Now, he forced his eyes open, unsure how long he'd been out.

Dylan was there, consoling Rebecca, who looked shaken to the core.

She caught Brody's gaze and locked on, immediately moving toward him. "Thank God, you're awake."

Brody tried to speak, but his mouth didn't immediately move. He took a few slow breaths and reset.

"What happened?" he managed to get out. Brody didn't even want to think about what would've happened to Rebecca if the others hadn't shown.

"He was here." One look at Rebecca's dilated pupils, her wide, fearful eyes, and Brody figured she'd retreated to that space deep inside her that no one could reach. He'd seen it a few times in high school and nothing good ever came of it. The most notable time was when she'd broken up with him.

"Did you guys get him?"

She shook her head. Damn if her disappointment and fear wasn't a sucker punch to his gut. Not to mention the way her hands shook when Dylan gave her a bottle of water.

"When did you guys get here?" Brody was still fuzzy. He remembered having a conversation with Ryan a little while ago.

"We were nearby. Called the sheriff as soon as we got here. They're searching the woods for him as we speak. We'd be out there, too, but—"

"Thank you for sticking around." His gaze immediately shifted to Rebecca.

"No problem, bro. She fought like a banshee. It's the only reason she's still here and not God knows where."

Dylan helped Brody sit up and handed him a bottle of water. "Did you get a good look at the guy?"

"He's tall and thin, but quick. She got the best view. He nailed me before I had a chance to react. He knows these woods." Brody glanced around, trying to get his bearings.

"Think you can help her work with a sketch artist?" Dylan asked.

"Yeah. I can try. Like I said, he practically cracked my skull in two when he surprised me, so mostly he looked like a tall, skinny blur." Brody made a move to get up but sat right back down when his head felt like someone had split it open with an ax. "Any idea what he used on me?"

"We're lucky it wasn't a gun."

Brody glanced at Rebecca, who stood there stiff, looking like she might jump out of her skin if someone said boo to her.

"Get her out of here."

She whirled around on him. Determination set her jaw. "No. I'm not leaving. Not without you."

"Ryan can take you to the ranch and stay with you there." He checked his head and came back with more blood on his hand. "I'm not getting up anytime soon."

She stood there, brown eyes piercing through him. "I'm not going anywhere."

"How long was I out?" Brody's gaze shifted from Rebecca to Dylan.

Dylan cleared his throat before he spoke. "Not long. I'd say we arrived within a few seconds of you blacking out."

Rebecca might be there, standing close, but a wall had gone up around her. Her muscles were stiff, her jaw tight, and her arms were crossed over her chest. Everything about her body language had changed. "I'm not leaving with you still here."

"She should be fine. We're all here," Ryan said as he walked over. "EMTs are close."

About that time Brody heard sticks crunching in the brush behind him, growing louder. "You guys can't stay here. This is the closest anyone's been to him. I'm fine and he can't be far. Go, get him. I'll pick up the search when I'm cleared."

Ryan's expression said he'd carry Brody to the hospital himself if he had to. Dylan was just as unmoving.

"Let the paramedics get here and take a look at you first. Then, we can go together," Ryan said.

Brody blew out a breath, closed his eyes and leaned back. They were saying that they didn't want him doing anything stupid, like not getting proper medical attention. "Fine. But I'm going out there." He motioned toward the thicket. Nausea gripped him as blood trickled down his nose. He didn't want to admit how close he was to passing out again. It was in that moment his drill sergeant's words chose to wind through his thoughts. The first rule of being a good soldier was to take care of injuries.

The next time Brody woke, he was in the back of an ambulance.

He blacked out again, then woke to the news he was in the hospital being treated for lacerations and a possible concussion. "How long was I out this time?"

"A half hour?" The muscles in Rebecca's face tensed and he could see her pulse thumping at her neck. She was stressed. As shaken as she was, and emotionally closed off, she'd refused to leave Brody's side. He didn't want to acknowledge what that did to his heart.

"What's going on? Is everyone okay?" he asked.

She thanked the nurse and then waited for the older woman to leave the room and close the door behind her. "No. You're seriously hurt. And it's my fault."

He put his hand up before she could get too worked up. "Hold on a minute. This has nothing to do with you."

"Yes. It does. I brought you into this mess and now look." When she turned to him a tear spilled down her cheek. Something quick and explosive hit his chest when she made eye contact.

"Sweetheart, none of this is on you. If anything, I should've been more careful in the woods. I should've realized he would know that area like the back of his hand. Plus, we got a look at him this time. The sheriff has a better description to work with. And that's a good thing, right?"

She nodded as a few more tears escaped. She quickly wiped them away.

"Look at me. I'm here because I made a mistake. I underestimated the situation. I won't do that twice. And, I'm going to be okay. Believe it or not, I have a pretty hard head."

At least that last comment got a smile out of her.

The haunted look in her eyes had returned, though. Brody had no idea how to break through that. He'd tried and failed before. Didn't figure much had changed since then. Even so, it was good to see her again. Better than he wanted to admit.

And that was most likely because he'd missed home, too. Being far off in a desert, away from everything familiar, had a way of playing tricks on a man's mind and making him weak. Brody reasoned that was why he still had residual feelings for Rebecca. She was "known," and it had nothing to do with the curve of her hips into those long legs. Or her laugh, which sounded like music to his ears. He had missed her quick mind, her will to live even under extreme circumstances. She'd felt like home to him years ago. Those feelings resurfaced and that's why his heart hurt being close to her.

"Where are Dylan and Ryan?"

"They stayed with the sheriff to help search the

thicket." She folded her arms. "Think I should call Alcorn? He might be able to get more resources out there."

"I want this guy caught, too, but that might not sit well with Ryan," Brody said.

"Right. I almost forgot how much they don't like each other." She rubbed her arms. "Besides, the guy is probably long gone by now."

"Dylan said something about a sketch artist."

"One is being sent over now." She glanced at her watch. "In fact, he should be here any minute."

REBECCA DIDN'T WANT to admit how great it felt to see Brody sitting up, awake, sipping water. Or how much she wished she could get closer to him, touch him again. But she wouldn't, for her sake as much as his. And especially because his compassion was evident in his words and actions, but that was all he felt for her. He'd been clear.

A knock on the door made her heart leap. Resentment hit fast and hard that an unexpected noise had that effect on her again, just like before, just like she'd sworn would never happen again.

Well, the bastard wasn't going to get away with it this time.

"Come in," she said, popping to her feet, needing to walk off her nerves.

An older gentleman with a sketch pad tucked under his arm walked in, accompanied by a deputy.

Brody was already up, sitting on the edge of the bed, which agitated the machines he was hooked up to. They beeped loudly.

The older nurse rushed in.

"Mr. Fields, you need rest."

"Do whatever you need to me while I'm here, but as

soon as this meeting is over, I'm walking out that door." He looked at Rebecca when he said, "Did you see my cell? I lost it back there."

She produced it and he took it from her, heat pulsing from where their fingers met.

"I wouldn't advise that. The doctor wants you to stay overnight for observation," the nurse warned.

"With all due respect, we're in the middle of an investigation and I don't have that kind of time."

She glared at him as she fiddled with dials, her gaze bouncing from him to the machine to Rebecca.

The deputy introduced both himself and the artist while Rebecca pulled extra chairs next to the bed. Brody made a move to help, but she motioned for him to stay put.

When the artist put the finishing touches on his sketch and showed it to her, dread wrapped around her shoulders. The finished product was still too vague. "That's not going to help. He's great at keeping his face hidden."

"It's a start," Deputy Holder said, and she could tell he was reaching. At least he wasn't looking at her as if she had six foreheads, half curious, half afraid, and expecting her face to explode. "We'll circulate this. See if we can't stir the pot a little."

At least the sheriff's office took her seriously now. She thanked the men and closed the door behind them.

The nurse turned toward Brody. "Any chance I can get you to change your mind and stick around a little while?"

"No." He shot an apologetic look. "I know you're doing your job, but I have to do mine."

The nurse gave an understanding nod before saying she'd be back and then leaving.

"I didn't get a good look at him." Rebecca sat on the edge of the bed, facing him without looking at him.

"This will help. The sheriff's office will start getting more leads than they can handle."

"It feels…hopeless." She threw her hands up in the air.

"One thing I learned on missions was to stay focused on a positive outcome no matter how bad things look. A thousand things can go wrong when you're out there, but thinking about them doesn't do any good. Positive thinking has more power to create change than I ever realized. If others knew how strong their minds were, people's lives would be very different."

"What did you focus on? What was home for you?"

He shifted his position, breaking eye contact. "I had a lot of things to come back to. Buying the ranch for one. My dad for another. Texas, my home."

A little piece of her heart wished he'd said her. But why would he? Not after the way she'd hurt him.

"Those are great things to keep you grounded." Rebecca had very little to keep her centered. She had her mother, whom she loved. What else did she have besides work and a couple of friends? Sadly, not much. Even her bungalow was a rental.

Her father was remarried with two boys, her half brothers, whom she'd never really been able to connect with no matter how much they'd tried. They weren't bad kids, but they weren't Shane, either. She could see the selfishness in those feelings now, but her teenage self had been less aware. And maybe it was her dad's new life that she never felt she fit into after he left.

Had Rebecca really made an effort?

Or had she expected him to go the extra distance to make her feel comfortable. He hadn't, so they'd drifted apart for a few years until she stopped visiting altogether.

There'd been so many people poking around in her

head, and all she'd wanted to do was be left alone and seem as normal as possible. Except she wasn't. She was damaged goods.

Had it been too easy to keep everyone at a safe distance? And now? What had changed?

Rebecca had taken over as her mother's caregiver, helping coordinate doctor appointments and medicines, and that had taken her mind off her own problems. A little part of her had been relieved not to be the focus for a change.

If she were being honest, she'd admit that being near Brody awakened pieces of her she'd ignored for so long.

"Did you bring the laptop?" Brody asked, breaking through her heavy thoughts.

"Yeah. I drove your truck."

"You thought to bring it to the hospital?" He glanced up, and what looked like pride was on his face.

Her heart fluttered. "I knew you wouldn't want to wait for someone to pick us up, so I drove. They wouldn't let me ride in the ambulance, anyway. I'll run down and get the laptop."

"That'll give us something to do while we wait for my release papers." He smiled.

She would never get used to the flush of warmth rolling through her at seeing him look so pleased with her. Maybe it was the way she'd left things all those years ago, the hurt in his eyes she remembered to this day, but she wanted Brody to be happy because of something she did.

It took all of ten minutes for her to retrieve the laptop and return. She set it on the bed, where Brody immediately opened the file.

"We recognize a face, get a name and maybe we get lucky with an address." Brody pulled up the list of suspects.

"There are so many familiar names. Do you remember who that is?" She pointed to the top name.

"Wasn't he our bus driver in middle school?"

"Yes." Her shoulders sank forward. "It makes me so sad to look at these names and think they might be such horrible people."

"We've known them most of our lives."

"If it's someone local, then they've hidden it for this long. There's no way they'd let this kind of secret out now."

"Don't be discouraged. No one's had this much information to go on before. We have a general description."

"It's still pretty vague," she pointed out.

"Once we narrow the list by height, we'll rule out a substantial amount of suspects. We know it can't be our bus driver. Mr. Alba was our height in middle school." His joke was meant to lighten her somber mood.

It helped. "True. Do you know how many men there are in Texas over six feet tall?"

"Yeah. We grow everything bigger in Texas." Brody laughed, and her tension eased. "Still, knowing this guy is six foot two will be a huge help."

"What if they were right all along? What if he was just passing through town all those years ago?"

"That's possible. Then we look outside of Texas."

"And what if this isn't him? What if it's some whack job imitating him?" She knew she was letting her fears get the best of her, but there were so many questions.

"Could be. But then we have to consider both sides of the coin."

"Okay, say we get a name. He'll surely go into hiding now. Not only did he slip out of my sight fifteen years ago, but he's done so twice today. No way will he stick around after this. How will we ever find him now?" Bile rose from her stomach, burning her throat. She wrung her hands and paced.

"I thought about all those things, too. We might keep looking and not find anything to go on. We might dig until we've dug to China and come up empty-handed. But it won't be for nothing. You'll know something. You'll know that you've given this your best shot. And that will help you put this to rest when the time comes." He held steady to her gaze. "First things first. We search these files while we give my pain a chance to ease and make sure I'm not going to pass out when I walk. Then, we head out and investigate. We don't stop until we find answers."

"And what if none of it helps?"

"It will."

She didn't respond, couldn't respond. She only wished she had his faith as she walked another ten steps to the window and back.

"Hey, come here."

She stopped, but her heart kept racing.

Brody patted the bed. "Let's look through this together. Maybe something else will stick out that the investigators missed before. You were closest to the scene and sometimes visuals help stimulate memories."

"Okay. You're right. Maybe we'll find something, and if we don't I'll figure out a way to live with it."

Rebecca's cell buzzed. She took the call, thanked the caller and then fixed her gaze on Brody.

"It's the nurse at the care facility. My mom needs me. I have to go."

Chapter Six

"Then let's go." Brody stood. His knee gave and he almost fell. He caught himself by grabbing hold of the chair.

"This is not a good idea. You should stay here until you're better. I'll go check on my mother and pick you up in a little while." She palmed the keys and slid her purse strap over her shoulder, giving the universal sign of a woman ready to go.

"Absolutely not, Rebecca. I will not leave you alone. You can drive, but I'm going with you." He'd regained his balance and looked steady on his feet. Steady and stubborn.

"The doctor hasn't released you yet, remember?"

"I'm not waiting around for someone to tell me to stay in bed for the next three days and rest. Besides, I'm better at assessing my injuries than anyone else. I know what my body can and can't handle."

She didn't want to think about why he knew how much punishment his body could take. Did it have to do with the three-inch scar running down his left arm?

He closed the laptop. "Besides, I can study the folder and make a few calls on the way to see your mother. That's the most efficient use of our time, anyway."

She stood there staring him down for a long moment.

He was in a weakened state and she wanted, no, needed him to get better.

And yet he had that determined set to his broad shoulders and prominent chin. His sturdy jawline anchored his steady gaze, which was fixed on the door.

When Brody Fields made up his mind about something, he followed through. Period. He could be as obstinate as a bull terrier and, injuries or not, just as lethal. No way was he listening to her.

The nurse shuffled into the room.

"Bring whatever paperwork you need to keep the lawyers off your back, but do it fast. You have about a minute before I walk out that door." He inclined his head toward the only exit in the room.

The nurse yelled out for someone and Rebecca assumed it was the floor supervisor.

"Forty-five seconds."

The woman blew out a frustrated breath. She stared him down before calling out the name again.

"Thirty."

A disgusted grunt came. "Fine. If you're determined to hurt yourself, I have no legal grounds to stop you. I'll get your paperwork. Stay right here."

"No, thanks. Time's up." Brody leaned forward. Everything about his body language said he was about to walk out that door.

"Will you stop by the nurse's station to sign a release form?"

Brody clenched the muscles in his jaw, nodded.

"Follow me."

SIGNING OUT TOOK all of ten minutes. Brody didn't want to give the nurse a heart attack, so he cooperated while she printed form after form and asked for his signature a dozen or more times.

Billing had decided to pay him a visit before he left, too. He'd given his credit card and signed for that, as well.

Once inside his truck, he checked in with Ryan. His friend had no news to report, which was expected since there hadn't been any texts or phone calls.

Dawson, another childhood friend, was tending to Brody's horses, so he gave him a ring, too. Last week Brody had gotten an injured stallion who might be ending his racing career. Lone Star Park kept him in horses that needed rehab. He also took in neglected animals. A dozen mares had been rescued days before dying from starvation because of an irresponsible breeder last month and they were doing nicely. He'd witnessed firsthand what humans could do to each other in war and at home. Seeing what they could do to animals hit him in a whole new place of frustration. Brody needed to check on his horses at some point this evening. There should be plenty of time to visit Mrs. Hughes and follow up on the restaurant lead they'd uncovered earlier.

"If it's not too late when we finish with your mother, I'd like to go to Mervin's tonight. See what we can find there, which might be nothing," he quickly warned.

"Okay. I don't think we should go alone, though."

Good point. He wasn't up to par in his weakened physical state. He was one more surprise attack away from being chained to a hospital bed with an IV that had something besides coffee in it. "I'll see which of the guys can go with us."

"I heard you invite them to Mother's," she said.

"Figured we could talk while you visit. I'm not going

inside her room, considering I'm pretty much the last person she'll want to see. I was never her favorite person."

"That was a long time ago."

"Some things don't change."

She broke into a smile. "True. But she'll tolerate pretty much anything if it means I'll spend more time there."

Brody shouldn't say what he was about to say, but he couldn't help himself. "You have the same shy smile you did in high school."

And the same eyes, serious and intelligent.

"Do I? Here I thought I'd grown up so much. Guess not."

"Not so fast. There's nothing wrong with looking like you're still in high school. Some women might even consider that a compliment." He laughed. "I'd like to see more of that thing curving your face, though."

"Oh, Brody. It's been so long since I…" The smile faded too quickly. So did the sparkle in her eye.

"Go ahead. Finish your sentence," he urged.

"It'll make me seem even sadder than I already am, especially to you."

"It won't. Come on. Tell me. Please."

She compressed her lips.

"I said 'please.'"

"Okay, fine. Have it your way. It's been so long since I had anything to really smile about."

He shook his head. "That's a damn shame. A woman as intelligent and kind as you, as beautiful as you, should have everything she wants. Love. Laughter. Children."

Rebecca shrugged.

"Don't tell me you never think about having a family someday." He couldn't hide his shock.

"Have it your way. I won't tell you, then." No hint of a smile on her face now.

"Seriously?" Didn't every little girl dream of having a fairy-tale wedding, a big house and kids? Brody didn't have siblings, so he couldn't speak from personal experience on what little girls dreamed of, but they'd been portrayed that way his whole life. "You never think about it?"

"Not really. Not since I was a little girl and unafraid of the big bad wolf. Now that I know wicked things happen to children and what that does to a parent, I can't think about going down that road as the mother. I've seen what it did to mine."

"I get that." He could see anguish fill her. If she didn't fight, it would swallow her whole.

"It's not so bad, you know." She tapped her finger on the steering wheel. "I'm used to being alone."

Those five words haunted him more than he wanted to admit. Was it because he was the same? Had she hit a personal note?

He mentally shook it off. This was not the best time for a conversation about having children, not when emotions from the past were being dredged up. Besides, the incident in the woods had sent Rebecca into an emotional tailspin. He'd seen that lost look on her face once. Right before she'd broken his heart. No matter how close they were, now or then, she'd never be able to meet him all the way. Whoa. Why was he thinking about the two of them in a present-day relationship?

It didn't matter. He still didn't have answers to her case. He was considering all the options and yet the simplest explanation, the one the Feds kept coming back to, was that the guy wasn't connected to Mason Ridge. If he had been, then Brody's job of finding the jerk would've been easier. The faster he could bring this monster to justice, the better. If only he could help bring peace to her family. The man responsible for Shane's disappearance needed to pay.

Brody had every intention of burying the bastard.

Time had come to get back to the basics in this case. He opened the laptop and then the file, studying it again as she drove toward Apple Orchard Care Facility, where her mother lived. The suspect list seemed never-ending. If he searched long enough, there had to be a connection somewhere. He'd been looking for an association to the town or the family. Maybe he needed to look harder for a link within their group of friends. Maybe Justin's friends.

"It's okay, you know," Rebecca finally said. "I'm not going to fall apart like my mother."

No. Rebecca was a survivor. Even after all these years, she kept her chin up, kept searching. "I know."

She stopped at a red light. "Why did you call the guys? I mean I know what you said, but there's more to it, isn't there?"

"I'm interested to see if anyone remembers anything."

"It was a long time ago, Brody. I doubt anyone besides me even thinks about it anymore."

The light changed and she pressed the gas.

There's where she was wrong. How could Brody forget? How could anyone forget who was there that night or in that town? He already knew Ryan had thought about it, as did Dylan and Dawson. That night was etched into everyone's memories.

Brody had called a secret meeting after Shane had disappeared. Rebecca couldn't be there, of course. But everyone else had shown. Parents had strictly forbidden kids to leave the house, so Samantha, Lisa and Melanie had arranged to be together, watched by Samantha's older brother. Every available adult was out on a search team, scouring fields and abandoned buildings. No one wanted to leave their children unattended after the incident. Brody's father had allowed him to join the search, so he hadn't needed an excuse to be out. Brody and the guys had sneaked inside Samantha's first-floor bedroom window, risking everything to meet.

None of their friends had admitted to seeing anything. Afraid of being busted, everyone had scattered. But had they been lying? Surely they'd seen something. Maybe if they talked it through again, as adults, a detail would pop.

Brody figured the real reason Rebecca couldn't let this go was because she'd yelled at Shane when the game broke up, humiliating him, so he ran to get away from her. The weight she carried was so much more than letting him down because she'd always watched over her little brother. At first, she'd told him to sit by a tree and wait. He didn't listen. She'd embarrassed him in front of her friends, telling him he had no business following her. Teary eyed, he'd broken into a full run, little athlete that he'd been. Even then, he'd been fast as a whip. And she'd completely underestimated him. By the time she'd apologized to everyone for her little brother ruining their mission, he was gone.

The bullet that was Shane had already disappeared out of view. Rebecca had told Brody that she wasn't worried about losing sight of her brother. He'd head home. Where else would he go?

A noise had spooked the rest of the group. The game had been a bad idea that night. There were too many people out after dark because of the festival. Afraid of getting busted, they'd scattered in different directions.

Brody had offered to help find Shane. Rebecca had said she'd be fine. A few minutes later, alone, she'd heard a muffled cry.

The rest was history.

And Brody felt responsibility, too. What if he'd insisted on helping her search? Would he have made a difference? Surely, the kidnapper wouldn't have been able to subdue three kids. Even at twelve, Brody had been substantial. He might have been the tipping point they'd needed. How many times had he asked himself that question?

It still didn't matter. Brody hadn't gone. Shane had been kidnapped. History couldn't be revised.

At twelve, Rebecca had been a tower of strength.

Even now, she dug her heels in and went full force chasing a lead rather than roll over. She threw herself into the investigation even if it meant shutting out everything else around her. But then, she'd been good at that before, too.

With her mother gravely ill, Brody wondered who Rebecca would have left after her mom was gone. Her father? They weren't close anymore. Was that part of why she'd clung to the idea that Shane could be alive? Fear of being alone?

Where did that leave Rebecca?

Brody wanted to be there for her, to see her through this now in a way he couldn't before. He hated the thought that she felt alone again, fighting for the life of someone in her family. She didn't need advice or someone to tell her what was best for her. He'd be there if she needed him, if she let him.

Watching her pain nearly killed him, but he knew the only way to put the past behind her was for him to be strong and, better yet, bring justice.

"Did you call your father back?"

"I've been with you every minute."

"I thought maybe you'd returned his call at the hospital when I was out."

"No. Not yet. I will, though." Her voice was unsteady, as if she was still trying to decide.

"When?"

"Soon."

"Why not now?"

"Can I ask you a question?" Rebecca's voice was far less frail and afraid than it had been earlier. He sensed that she was gaining her strength. She might've been shell-shocked, but she wasn't broken. Not even the Mason Ridge Abductor could take that away from her.

Too many places inside him needed Rebecca to be okay.

"Yeah. Sure."

"What happened with your mother? I mean, I've heard the rumors about her convincing the town to invest in a lakefront resort and then disappearing with the money. That true?"

"Yes."

"Does it still bother you?"

"No." Brody had hoped this one time that she couldn't read his mind. They'd shared a mental connection in high school that had him wondering if dating her had been a good idea. He wasn't sure he wanted someone to understand the pain he was in. He was a kid, and he'd been feeling sorry for himself.

"Are you in contact with her?"

"No."

"Why not?"

"Other than the fact that she hasn't tried to get in

contact with me once since she left? I don't have anything to say to her."

"That all? You can be honest with me, Brody. I won't tell anyone. Not like I have a bunch of people to tell, anyway…" Her words trailed off at the end and he could tell she tried to come off as unaffected by the truth in those words. "It's more than that, isn't it? You value family."

Did he? He'd spent his teen years bitter about his mother's actions, his father's lack thereof. "I value loyalty more."

"That, too. But you never talk about her. I mean, you must feel something. Like with my dad, I was angry with him for starting another family. Especially since this one felt so…unfinished."

"Have you forgiven him? Moved on?"

"I guess not. But I am trying."

"Really? How so? By not answering his calls?" He glanced at her in time to see regret darken her features. Damn. He didn't expect her reaction to hit him so hard.

"I deserve that." Chin up, she seemed ready for another punch.

"That wasn't fair of me—"

"Yes, it was. I'm the one who brought up the subject. I shouldn't dish it out if I can't take it, right?"

"I still didn't mean it."

"Don't worry. I get it. You're doing the same thing I do. Push those feelings down so deep that no one can touch them. They're buried. They can't hurt you. But, lately, I've been wondering if that's the right thing to do."

"Meaning you want to call your father." Was she right? Brody had done his level best to forget the feelings existed.

"For one. I mean, part of me wants to talk to him. The rest thinks it's too late to start our relationship now."

"He wouldn't try to get in touch if he didn't want to spend time with you. My situation's different. My mom took off and that was it. I never heard from her again. No birthday cards. No surprise high school graduation visit. She hasn't tried to get in touch once. And it's bad enough she stole from the town, but look what she did to my father. He never stopped waiting for her to come back, never got over her. She had to know how much he loved her, I loved her. And not one word in more years than I can count. Not exactly a person worth tracking down." Anger had those last words biting out. He never talked about his mother, not to anyone. He'd convinced himself that he no longer cared about her or the way she'd treated his father. Was that true? The venom he felt surging through him said otherwise. Was it good to dredge up the past?

"You're right. You're completely right. Our situations are totally different. But our way of dealing with them is pretty much the same." She hesitated. "I'm glad you talked about it. You never used to."

"Like I said, wasn't much to say before."

"And now?"

"Talking to you is different. We have history." It was more than that, but no way would he allow himself to dwell on that emotion. He didn't need to know how deep his feelings ran for Rebecca. The bottom line was that she'd shut him out just as his mother had. And Brody was nothing like his father. Brody wouldn't sit around licking his wounds, waiting for a woman who could so easily walk away from him to return.

He shoved those thoughts aside as Rebecca pulled into

a parking spot and cut the engine. "I'll stick around out here and keep digging in these files while you go inside."

She lightly touched his hand, and even that little bit of contact sent sparks flying. Another reminder it was a bad idea to get too close to her this time around. Sparks ignited flames. Unchecked, flames developed into full-blown fires. A raging fire destroyed everything in its path. Just like his mother had. And his father had simply stood in its way and gotten burned.

But Rebecca's situation with her father couldn't be more different. "It's okay to love your father, you know."

"I do now. But by the time I realized it, his calls had slowed and it just seemed easier to leave things alone. Sleeping dog and all that. Now I'm thinking maybe I just took the coward's way out."

"You? Not a chance." Brody shook his head. He brushed against her right cheek with the backs of the fingers on his left hand. "You're one of the strongest people I've ever known."

She smiled, warming him, warning him that getting too close to fire would engulf him just like it had his father. Brody wasn't objective when it came to Rebecca. And that was dangerous.

"I'm sorry about your family, Brody." Her look was all compassion and sympathy, creating an intimacy between them he didn't want to acknowledge, and it stirred something in his chest he had no desire to think about.

"I guess there's no chance I can convince you to come inside with me."

The others hadn't arrived yet. Brody texted them to say that he had. A second later, he got a message that the guys would be running late. Dylan had to swing by and check on Maribel who wasn't feeling well. "I doubt your mother wants to see me."

"You might be surprised." She unbuckled her seat belt and reached for the handle. "Why not see for yourself."

"Hold on a sec." Hopping out of the truck, his knee giving in the process, he steadied himself and rounded the front end, determined to open the door for her. Part of him wanted to be there for Rebecca, to hold her hand through it all, but the other part—the logical one—said going inside with her was a bad idea since he didn't want to upset her mother with his presence. Then again, the thought of Rebecca going anywhere alone didn't sit well, either.

Rebecca held out her hand.

Brody took it, ignoring how well hers fit.

"I know you're supposed to meet the guys out here, but will you go in for a minute?" she asked.

If she hadn't asked, he sure as hell wouldn't have volunteered. She had. Against his better judgment, he nodded.

She smiled and that annoying part of his heart stirred again. Sure didn't take much to get that going. *Way to be strong, Fields.*

But he was expert at swallowing his true feelings. Rebecca was no exception. Pretending he hadn't just told himself a big fat lie, he held out his arm for her.

The next touch, her hand to his forearm, was so light it barely registered. The electricity it sent up his arm was another story altogether. Frissons swirled up his arm, lighting a path straight to his chest. And he suppressed the thought that no other woman had that effect on him, chalking it up to unrequited love. Because if her feelings had run a fraction of his, then she wouldn't have been able to walk away all those years ago, would she? Unlike his father, Brody had no intention of being the fool twice. Between her and his mother, he was beginning to feel destined to associate with women who had no problem walking away from him. Wouldn't Freud have a field day with that one?

The facility was small and well kept. Purple and pink flowers lined the path to the front door of the two-story brick building. A large pot of flowers flanked each side of the oak door and white rocking chairs lined the oversize porch.

"You're sure this is a good idea? Me going inside?" Rebecca's mother had made her feelings toward Brody clear years ago, saying he wasn't good enough for her daughter. The fact that his mother later stole from the town hadn't improved his standing with Mrs. Hughes, even though he'd had nothing to do with it. Still, he didn't imagine her feelings had changed.

"I want you there."

"With her condition, I don't want to make things worse."

"It won't. She's changed a lot. For so many years she was afraid something else would happen to me. She didn't want me to leave the house for fear I wouldn't walk back in the door. Her feelings toward you back then had little to do with you and so much to do with everything else she was dealing with." Rebecca paused, stopping a few steps in front of the door. "Besides, she asks about you."

Well, didn't that last comment stop him in his tracks? "Me?"

The shy smile returned. "Yep. I know she wasn't nice to you back then, but if you could forgive her. I know it would mean the world to her."

"Already done. I don't have kids of my own, but I can only imagine what that's like after seeing Dylan with

Maribel. Hell, I'd give my life for that little girl and she's not even mine. I understand where your mom is coming from."

Rebecca didn't immediately start walking again. Instead, she turned to Brody. The equivalent of a thunderstorm brewed behind her eyes. "I think she held on for so many years to the hope my brother would come back alive. Now, she's suffering. Her body wants to go, but she can't. I think it's because she never found closure. A little piece of her half expects him to come walking through the door at any moment."

"Because they never found out what happened to him?"

She nodded. "Mom's just this shell of a person, hanging on. And I know it sounds awful, but I just wish she could find peace. I wish she could let go. She's so tired. Her mind is going. Sometimes she talks about him like he's still here. Yet, she hangs on."

The reason Rebecca wanted Brody with her made a little more sense now. Based on the anguish on her face, she was barely holding on, too. If she needed him to be strong for her, to get through this, he could do that. For her. For him. As a tribute to their past.

Without thinking much about it, he hauled her against his chest. She buried her face as he dipped his head and whispered in her ear. "It's okay. I'm here. Nothing else bad is going to happen."

She gave in to the moment, softening her body against his. And Brody couldn't help but notice for the second time how well they fit. This close, he could feel her heartbeat increasing and the smell of her shampoo, that same mix of citrus and flowers, engulfed his senses.

There was nothing more or less that he could do then except cup her cheeks in his hands and guide her lips to his. Kissing her felt like home. Light at first, deepened when she opened her mouth for him and slid her tongue inside. Her fingers tunneled into his hair as the urgency of the kiss amplified.

Brody's logical mind said she was seeking temporary shelter in a storm. As soon as this blew over, they'd be right back where they started.

With great effort, he pulled back first. "We'd better head down the hall. Since the guys are running late, I might just tell them to meet us at the restaurant in a little while."

Too quickly, her composure returned, her body stiffened. "You're right. I'm sorry."

"Don't apologize. I probably enjoyed that more than you did."

"I doubt it. And that's not where we need to be right now."

Didn't that confuse him till the cows came home? It had to be a strain to hold so much weight on her shoulders. "You know we're going to figure this out, right? You don't have to do this alone. I'm here. The guys are helping. Law enforcement's involved. He's not going to get away with this."

"I have to find him before he gets to me again, Brody."

A foreboding feeling tugged at him. "I know."

Chapter Seven

Rebecca clasped her hand around Brody's as they turned toward her mother's wing. Warmth spread through her from the contact and she didn't fight it. Instead, she relaxed into it, letting it drift through her, calming her, grateful to have Brody's support even if that's where the connection between them had to end—at friendship.

As they rounded the corner to her mother's hallway, she saw a couple hovering. A man she immediately recognized as the reporter who'd hassled her at her car stood behind them, looking down. Was that jerk trying to hide?

Rebecca squeezed Brody's hand.

He glanced at her, must've seen the shock on her face and tucked her behind him.

The couple looked at Rebecca in unison, their faces pale and desperate. Their gazes were intent as the woman rushed toward Rebecca.

"Ms. Hughes?" The panicked look on the woman's face said everything Rebecca needed to know as to why the lady was there. The expression was unmistakable, hope mixed with anxiety and fear. Gaunt eyes. Sallow skin.

"You want to get out of here?" Brody asked her quietly, his large frame blocking her view.

"Yes." She turned back toward the hallway they'd come from.

"Please, don't go." The woman's voice was full of terror. "It's our son. He's been missing since last year and we were hoping you could help. We're from Sunnyvale."

Hearing those words nearly ripped Rebecca's heart out again. Whatever had happened, Rebecca feared she wouldn't be able to help. She'd tried with her brother's case and look how well that had turned out. "I'm so sorry. I wish there was something I could do."

The woman's brows knit in confusion. "Peter Sheffield called and told us what happened." Brody took several steps forward, making progress toward her mother's door, using his body as a shield. He squeezed Rebecca's hand and she realized he was bringing her closer to her mother's room. She understood his message. Once she got close enough, she could duck inside and lock the door. Later, she'd have a conversation with security about how the reporter brought a couple into what was supposed to be a secure facility.

"It'll just take a minute of your time," the man Rebecca assumed was the father said. He had that same look—dark circles under his eyes, desperation written across his features.

Rebecca glanced at the reporter. Sheffield was tall and sinewy. He had the beady eyes of a rat. Why was he here? What kind of game was he playing?

"I'm sorry that Mr. Sheffield said I could help in some way. I'm afraid he's wrong." Rebecca had made a fatal mistake in making eye contact with the desperate mother. No way could Rebecca slip away now. Those eyes would torment her for the rest of her life if she didn't face the woman.

"He was seven. Just like your brother," the mother quickly added.

Brody's body stiffened as he folded his arms across his chest.

She touched his arm, moved around him, and whispered, "It's okay."

His brow went up when she passed him. He didn't make a move to stop her.

Meeting with a mother who was facing her worst nightmare head-on sent a jolt, like a shotgun blast, through Rebecca's chest. If there was anything she could say or do to ease this woman's pain, Rebecca would. "What do you think I can do to help?"

Sheffield pulled a small device from his pocket, no doubt ready to record everything he heard.

Rebecca shot a look toward Brody. He immediately bumped into Sheffield, mumbling an apology, knocking the recording device out of his hand. "Oops. Didn't mean to do that. Let me help you pick it up."

"No. I got it," Sheffield said, irritated.

Brody scooped up the device and took the battery out. He handed the small piece of metal over to Sheffield with a look that dared him to complain.

The woman's gaze flashed from Rebecca to Brody. "I'm so sorry to bother you. It's just we heard about your situation and we thought you might be able to help us."

"I'd like to, but I'm not sure what I can do. I have my hands full caring for my mother right now and my brother's case is fifteen years old." She was careful not to reveal too much, or talk about what she was really working on.

"You're the only one who knows what we're going through." The mother who was in her mid-to-late thirties wrung her hands together. Her light brown eyes were red rimmed and dull, the sense of helplessness and despair written all over the dark circles underneath. She was small framed and looked as if she hadn't eaten in days. With her long brown hair and big eyes, she would be considered attractive under normal circumstances.

Her husband looked to be just under six feet with a runner's build, light hair with blue eyes. He had that same haunted look on his face, the one so familiar to Rebecca. He stood off to the side, looking hopeless and helpless. Everything about his body language said he needed to bring his child home.

Rebecca tried to speak, to find some words of encouragement for the desperate couple, but none came.

"Why don't you tell us your son's name?" Brody interjected.

"Jason." The woman took a step forward and her knees buckled. Before she hit the floor, Brody was on one side of her, her husband on the other. She looked up at him and a tender look passed between them. The gesture tugged at Rebecca's heart.

The love and concern on the couple's faces, their tenderness toward each other, outlined just how much love they shared. Had Rebecca's parents ever felt that way toward each other?

They'd grown up in a small town, had been high school sweethearts and married after he graduated college, as everyone had expected. They had history, had tried to be there for each other. But Rebecca wondered if they'd ever had *real* love like this. Her father had it now. She'd seen it with his second wife. A piece of her had been sad and it made her feel even more out of place at his house, like Christmas wrapping paper left over from the year before. Useful, but not exactly what he wanted anymore.

"Take her into my mom's room. I'll get a nurse," Rebecca said to Brody, grateful her voice had returned. There had to be something she could do to help this sweet couple.

Sheffield tried to follow, but Rebecca held her hand out. "Absolutely not. Not you."

The two men carried the woman, stopping to gently lower her into the chair near Rebecca's mother, who had propped herself up when they entered the room, her gaze traveling over the faces.

Rebecca touched her mother's arm. "I'll explain in a minute and then we'll talk about why you called."

The woman apologized several times before Rebecca could reassure her that it was all right. Her mother looked no worse than usual and Rebecca wondered if the call was a stunt for attention.

Mother responded with a blank look.

If Mother hadn't had the nurse call, then it had to have been Sheffield.

Brody disappeared to escort the reporter out of the building.

"Sometimes, I just walk into a room and it's like all the air gets sucked out and the world tilts. I get dizzy. I'm so sorry," the woman repeated.

Rebecca sat across from the woman on the edge of her mother's bed, listening.

A nurse hurried in and examined the woman. "Everything looks fine. A doctor will be in to check on you in a minute."

"No," the woman said, waving away the nurse, "I'll

be okay. I just need a second to catch my breath and a glass of water."

Brody walked in, a confused look on his face.

"I'm sorry. Where are my manners? I'm Kevin Glenn, and this is my wife, Chelsea." He shook Brody's extended hand and then Rebecca's. "Our son disappeared last year. We spoke to law enforcement, FBI, and they haven't been able to find him."

"We know exactly how you feel," Rebecca's mother said, her chin out and determination in her gaze. "And we know exactly what you're going through. Come. Sit." She patted the bed near her, looking stronger than she had in months. "This is a lot to have thrown at you at once. Believe me, I understand."

Rebecca scooted down so that Kevin could sit next to her mother.

"Mrs. Hughes, I'm so sorry for your loss," he said, choking back a tear.

"Thank you," her mother replied. "What happened to us tore our family apart. I made a lot of mistakes. There comes a time when you have to focus on what you have left." Mother glanced from Brody to Rebecca. "And hope it's not too late."

Rebecca smiled at her mother.

Kevin's shoulders rocked as he swiped away tears. "I apologize for barging in like this. It's just when we heard about what happened to you this morning, we wondered if the kidnappings could be related. Sheffield had reached out to us to write an anniversary story on our son's disappearance. We haven't been speaking to the media, but then he said he thought our story might be related to yours somehow and that got our attention. Then he told us you had some kind of an accident in the woods. We've been waiting here ever since."

"We did and we reported it to the sheriff's office," Rebecca said, while holding her mother's gaze.

"You were with Sheriff Brine in the woods?" Mother gasped and brought her hand up to cover her heart.

"It was one of his deputies, but yes."

"What were you doing...*there*?"

"It's a long story, Mother. I don't want you to worry about me. I'm completely fine." Rebecca tried to smooth it over, but her mother's wild eyes said words weren't helping.

"You shouldn't have been there, Rebecca. You should let the sheriff's office do its job."

"They haven't done it so far."

"There's nothing else you can do. You have to let it go." Fear and panic raised her voice several octaves. All her mother's protective instincts seemed to flare at once. A spark lit her eyes as she sat up as straight as she could manage.

Rebecca moved to the side of her mother's bed, not wanting to rile her. Too much agitation wouldn't be good for her heart. "No. I can't. And not just because I want to find out what happened to Shane. The man is back and he's trying to hurt me. I can't allow it. And if I can find out what happened before...then I owe it to you and me to do so now."

"Don't do it for me. You don't owe me anything, dear. It's not safe for you out there. I'll talk to the doctor about making space for you here." This was the most life Rebecca had seen from her mother in years. A piece of Rebecca wanted a reaction from her mother just to know that she was still alive in there. Usually, she stayed in bed day after day, watching TV and sleeping. Her daily exercise routine consisted of six trips to the bathroom.

"I understand why you'd panic. I didn't mention it to upset you." Rebecca held her mother's hand. The iciness was gone now. Hot, angry blood ran through her veins.

"Rebecca, be reasonable. You can't go out there while he's around. What if he comes after you again? I can't do anything from this bed. I can't protect you from here."

Her mother's blood pressure was increasing to unhealthy levels. "I hear what you're saying, but I have protection."

Her mother's gaze shifted from Rebecca to Brody and back. "No one can save you against a monster like that."

"The best thing you can do to help me is calm down." Her mother's eyes were wild now and her breaths came out in short bursts. Her gaze darted around the room, landing on the Glenns and then Brody. "Not even you will be able to stop him. No one could before."

Brody took a knee beside her bed, lowering himself to eye level. "Nothing will happen to your daughter as long as there's air in my lungs."

Tense, Rebecca readied herself for the fight that was sure to come.

"The best thing you can do for your daughter is trust her, trust me." He took hold of her mother's hand and held on to it.

Instead of responding with anger, she blew out a breath. Her shoulders slumped forward and, for the first time, she looked almost relieved. "I know you're right. My girl is smart. She's a lot tougher than I ever was."

"No one blames you for your reaction. Hell, I'd be the same way," Brody continued, his voice a calm port in the sea of tension that had been surrounding them. "And no one should have to go through what you did."

Her mother eased back onto her pillow, keeping a tight grip on Brody's hand. "I was worried about her. That's the reason I called. I'm glad she has you, Brody."

"We have a chance to find him. To know about…" Brody didn't immediately finish his sentence. "That's why Rebecca and I went to the woods. And, yes, we were attacked, but she fought that creep off until help arrived."

"You were close to him?" Her mother's eyes were now wide blue orbs.

"Yes, Mother," Rebecca said. "I had to be. He won't be out there much longer. The sheriff can't ignore me anymore. He'll get him this time. And if he doesn't, we will."

The excitement looked to be taking a toll on her mother. Her gaunt features paled as she suppressed a cough. She had the disposition of a deployed airbag.

"You should rest. Keep up your strength." Rebecca might not be able to bring her brother back, but she could help find the man who had taken Shane from them. She didn't have the heart to think *Shane's killer*. The small sprig of hope that had refused to die inside her had prevented her from doing so. Hope that the young man she'd located on social media would turn out to be Shane. Hope that she hadn't wasted more than half of her life searching for a brother she would never find.

Had she funneled all her energy into finding him in order to avoid acknowledging his death?

Kevin made a move to stand. Her mother caught his arm with her free hand. "Stay."

"We don't want to intrude. Your daughter's right. You should rest," he said. "We were foolish to show up like this. Sheffield said you could help. I'm really sorry. Your family has been through enough already."

"Will you keep me company for a while?" Her mother's voice, frail and tired, trailed off at the end of her question.

Kevin nodded as she closed her eyes.

"You don't have to," Rebecca whispered just out of her mother's earshot.

"We don't mind. It's just the two of us now. If it's okay with you, we'd like to stay here. I know it's going to sound weird, but it's nice, for a change, to be with people who understand. Who don't look at us like we're about to freak out or break."

"Believe me, I do get that." Rebecca reached out and patted Chelsea's hand.

Mother smiled softly. "It's nice to have company."

Brody's cell buzzed. He excused himself and disappeared into the hall.

When he returned, the look on his face said the others had arrived.

"We'll check in on you guys later," Rebecca said.

As she walked toward the door, Chelsea touched her arm. "Good luck with your search. Will you let us know if you find anything?"

"Absolutely." Rebecca was grateful they were with her mother. The slight rattle to her breathing made her fear her mother didn't have much time.

"WHEN YOU CAME back into Mother's room earlier, you looked confused. What happened?" Rebecca asked.

She didn't miss a trick. Or did she just read Brody that well? Probably both. He'd work toward being less transparent next time.

"I went out to see to if our friend found the front door all right. He was too easy to escort out."

"So he got frustrated and left."

"I'm not so sure. Think about it. First, he brings that couple to you. Why?"

"Because he's been dying to get an interview with me."

"Exactly. And he had you right there. But then he left? Have you ever seen a reporter give up on a story so easily?"

"Good point. He went to all the trouble to make sure the Glenns came to see me. He wouldn't leave like that, would he?"

"And that's another thing that bugs me. How did he know where you'd be?"

"I need to ask my mother if he spoke to her before. I'm thinking he tricked the nurse and prompted her call."

"That's true. And he also told the Glenns about the attack in the woods. How did he know about that?"

Rebecca shrugged. "Who knows how reporters figure things out? Sources, I guess."

"And that could be anybody."

"He might have a contact at the sheriff's office. When we called it in they could've let him know."

"I just wonder what else he thinks he knows. He wouldn't have left here if he didn't think there was a hotter story or lead somewhere else." Brody didn't like the way the reporter had tried to bully Rebecca. He made a mental note to keep an eye on the guy.

The fact that Sheffield seemed to be watching their movements didn't sit well. Then again, maybe he was trying to make a name for himself. Solving the case the sheriff couldn't would be a huge boost to the guy's career.

THE RIDE TO MERVIN'S EATS was quiet. Dawson's black sport utility was parked in the lot.

"The place is busy. I wonder if any of Randy's friends will be here." Rebecca's expression was easy to read. Her wide gaze was more desperate than hopeful.

"There's a slim chance we'll get a hit on the first try, right? Let's get a feel for the place. See if we think it's a good idea to ask around. Someone might know something."

"They wouldn't likely tell strangers, would they?"

"We'll make something up." Brody scratched the scruff on his chin. It was long past dinnertime and had been a full day. He could use a hot shower and a warm bed. Thoughts of the kiss he'd shared with Rebecca edged into his mind. He pushed them away. "Ready?"

Rebecca took in a deep breath and grabbed the door handle. "Let's go."

Ryan hopped out of Dawson's SUV first, followed by Dylan and Dawson.

After hugs and greetings were exchanged, the five of them moved inside.

The place was a decent size and had a nice hometown feel to it. Lots of autographed snapshots of a man who Brody assumed was the owner with professional athletes and musicians lined the walls.

A surprising number of people filled the place given dinnertime had come and gone a good three hours ago. There was still plenty of seating for more. Brody stopped at a sign that read Please Wait to Be Seated.

Music played in the background, but it wasn't loud enough to drown out the buzz of lively conversation. The place was about half-full.

A hostess wearing form-hugging jeans and a Mervin's

Eats T-shirt greeted them. She checked them out and smiled. "Just five tonight or are you expecting more?"

Rebecca looked to Brody for a response.

"We're all here," he said.

"Do you want menus? The kitchen's open another half hour," she said, twirling her hair and leaning toward Brody.

He looked to the guys, who seemed about ready to bust out laughing. They shook their heads.

"Just two."

"Well, then, follow me." She pulled the requisite number of menus, flashed a smile and spun toward the grouping of tables to her left. She paused long enough to ask, "Booth or table?"

"We're not picky," Brody responded.

Another smile came and this time her cheeks flushed.

Rebecca elbowed him as he let her pass him to take the lead. Her eyebrows pinched together as though she were scolding him.

Now it was Brody's turn to try to hold back a laugh. If she'd noticed, then the hostess was most definitely flirting.

And, if he was being honest, his reaction would've been much worse if the tables had been turned. Even so, he put up his hands in the universal sign of surrender and whispered, "I didn't do anything."

The others jabbed him in the shoulder and arm as they walked past.

Ryan was last. "How's Rebecca?"

"Strong. I don't have to tell you what she's been through."

Ryan nodded as they approached the round corner booth. Each one filed in to the right.

Brody slid left, so he could sit next to Rebecca. He

liked having her positioned in between him and one of the guys. Anyone wanting to get to her would have to go through one of them first. Brody also liked the idea of having backup. The light dose of pain medication from the hospital was wearing off and a freakin' jackhammer pounded the spot between his eyes.

A waitress stopped by to take drink orders. Brody ordered chicken-fried steak with iced tea and smiled when Rebecca did the same. The others ordered an appetizer of chicken wings and a round of beers. Normally, Brody would join them, but tonight he wanted a clear head. Whoever was after Rebecca could strike at any time. Brody figured the guy wouldn't be stupid enough to try anything with the others around, especially since they were all big guys and this creep only struck like a coward. He didn't fight head-on. He hid in the trees, in the brush, the element of surprise his only advantage. His preferred target had been a child.

The thought of the Sunnyvale boy going missing last year near the anniversary of Shane's disappearance weighed heavily on Brody's mind.

When the waitress had thanked them and disappeared, he clasped his hands and intentionally kept his voice low. "It means a lot to both of us that you guys are here. We're hoping to connect with the whole group, but the girls have spread out so that's a bit trickier on short notice. Samantha's in Dallas."

"And Lisa moved a couple of counties over," Ryan added. "Anyone know where Melanie is?"

Dawson nodded. "I ran into her sister the other day. She moved to Houston, and never comes back to visit. I think she stays in touch with Samantha and Lisa, though. I can check with one of them."

Brody thanked Dawson for helping out with the horses earlier.

"Do you guys still hang out?" Rebecca asked.

Most shook their heads.

"That's such a shame. We were all so close when we were little. Remember how long we used to play outside?" Rebecca asked.

"Remember Red Rover?" Dylan chimed in.

Heads nodded and smiles returned.

"Sad that we didn't stay that way. It's my fault," Rebecca said.

"Everyone's to blame, not just you," Dawson quickly interjected. "We were kids. No one knew what to say or do. We were all scared. Looking back, I feel like we let you down."

"You didn't," Rebecca said. "I was out of school for a year and my parents didn't let me see anyone. I missed you guys, but everything was so crazy for such a long time. I think I forgot how to have friends."

The waitress arrived with drink orders and the appetizers, momentarily stopping conversation.

"All our parents flipped out after that. Everyone changed. *Everything* changed. And none of it was your fault, Rebecca. We wish we would've gone searching with you that night. If we had, things would've been different." Dylan lifted his mug. "The reason stinks, but we're together now. So, glasses up."

How many times had Brody had the exact same thought? Too many, he thought, as he lifted his glass.

Ryan leaned forward, his serious expression returned.

"Justin is grateful for everyone covering for him that night. I don't know if I ever thanked you guys for that."

"Sheriff Brine really had it in for your brother after he got caught breaking into school," Brody said.

"My brother was stupid back then," Ryan said. "He learned his lessons the hard way. Besides, the sheriff couldn't hurt Justin any worse than what he got at home."

Brody remembered that Justin had stayed out of school beyond his week's suspension when he'd been caught. The beating he'd received from his father had left permanent marks on the backs of his legs. "We all knew covering for him was the right thing to do."

"I appreciate it," Ryan said.

"Speaking of the sheriff's office, my friend gave me a copy of the Mason Ridge Abductor's file. According to the FBI profiler, he would most likely have had a job that required him to travel around the state."

"Like a festival worker?" Dawson asked.

Brody nodded. "They ruled out local bus drivers, shop owners, and everyone else with a stable job."

"I remember how adamant the sheriff was about this being a transient worker. Didn't they check out everyone connected to the festival?" Dylan asked.

"They did," Rebecca said. "But there are so many people who come through town this week for the activities. The RV park by the Mason Ridge Lake is completely booked. Has been for months. And it's like that every year. There are workers but then also tons of people who come just for the festival. It's impossible to keep track of everyone."

"So, they're saying it was most likely someone here for the festival and not necessarily someone who works there," Dylan clarified.

"Right," Brody said. "But here's the thing. The Mason Ridge Abductor was smart enough not to get caught, which took some doing. But then lower-IQ offenders are the ones who tended to spend time in jail. This guy has avoided capture for fifteen years. He didn't have to be especially brilliant, just smart enough to cover his tracks. He could be one of us."

"Are you saying you don't think law enforcement had it right before?" Dylan asked.

"The more I think about the facts in this case, the more I believe someone right here could've been involved." Seeing Rebecca's brown eyes look weary and pained caused Brody to clench his hands. He hated everything about this case, except the part about seeing Rebecca again. Even so, watching her expression, knowing how much she was hurting, felt like a clamp around his heart. "There's a reporter who is hot on the case. You guys remember Peter Sheffield?"

"He's a jerk," Ryan said. "But harmless. I heard he's trying to make a name for himself at the paper."

Brody had figured as much. He hoped the guy didn't get in their way.

Rebecca turned to him, a wishful look in her eyes. "Should we tell them about Randy?"

The others exchanged looks.

"Rebecca has been searching social-media sites and she came across someone who looks a lot like Shane. There are pictures online of him hanging out with friends here," Brody said. He fished his phone from his pocket and pulled up the social media site. He located the pictures and passed his phone around the table.

"He has the same chin as Rebecca," Dawson observed.

"That why we're meeting here?" Ryan asked, studying the photo.

Brody nodded.

"Good idea," Ryan said, his gaze shifting to the hostess. "Friendly place."

Brody knew that his friend was referring to her flirting. In fact, she'd kept her eye on the table and a smile on her face ever since. Rebecca seemed to notice, too.

Chapter Eight

Rebecca didn't realize she'd been holding her breath until Ryan returned. He'd offered to fish for information from the hostess, giving Brody an out so he wouldn't have to be the one to do it. "What did she say?"

He slid inside the booth. "She recognized him but didn't know him personally. Said he hasn't been in for months, though."

"Did she have a guess as to why?" Rebecca asked.

"I'm afraid not."

"What about his friends? Do they still come in?" she quickly added.

"Negative, but she wasn't surprised. Said groups of young people come and go, many of whom head off to college. A lot of them find jobs in bigger cities after school since professional jobs are scarce around here. Others go into the military."

Her chest felt like a balloon with a hole in it, slowly leaking air—and hopes of finding Shane along with it.

Brody perked up with the news. "The first place we'll check is the military. It'll be easy to find him if he enlisted."

Dylan nodded. "I have a contact, too."

A burst of optimism spread across the men's faces.

Rebecca, on the other hand, felt she was back at square one.

The food arrived, stalling conversation once more. After hearing the disappointing news, she was grateful to be able to fix her attention on eating.

It was probably too good to be true that Shane had grown up a couple towns away, safe, in a good home. If he couldn't be with her and her mother, she'd at least wished he'd be well cared for and happy. He was so young when he'd been taken she wondered if he would remember her at all. She'd read in an article a few years ago that people retained very few memories before age ten. Shane had been seven, well below the age of retention. Her own memories of him had faded over the years. If she hadn't had photographs of him everywhere, would she remember him at all? Being the oldest, she had to believe she would.

A strange thought struck. What if she found him and he rejected her? What if he didn't want to go back? What if he was perfectly satisfied with his life?

Could he be completely happy without ever knowing about his past? Was it selfish to want to force that on him if by some miracle she found him alive?

One thing was certain. Rebecca had to know what had happened to her baby brother. She prayed he was thriving. And if he was, when she saw him, knew he was fine, then she'd decide if she had any right to intrude on his life.

Dealing with her mother complicated the situation. On the one hand, her mother had a right to know about her son. On the other, Shane or Randy or whatever his name was deserved to live in peace, if that was the case.

Rebecca took a bite of chicken-fried steak and chewed.

Brody leaned toward her, his arm touching hers. He seemed to realize she'd gone inside her thoughts, gotten lost there. In barely a whisper, so only she could hear, he said, "This is good. We're making progress."

In difficult times she'd learned that it was best to focus on the here and now. Besides, he was right. They knew more than they had in years. And even if Randy wasn't Shane, at least they could rule him out. Progress. They were making progress. Progress would be her new mantra. She'd already learned the hard way that dwelling on the negative only brought her down further.

And with the guys back together, she was beginning to believe that anything was possible.

When the plates had been hauled away, she thanked them for coming.

"Is there anything else you recall from that night? Anything we need to be on the lookout for?" Dylan asked.

"The thing I remember the most is strange," she said. "It's a smell. Apple tobacco."

"That was never in the papers," Ryan said quickly.

Something flashed in his expression that sent a chill scurrying up her spine. Recognition? She carefully studied him. "The FBI wanted to keep it out of the news. They were already bombarded with leads and they said the more information we gave the bigger chance we had of copycats and false leads. Why?"

"It would've helped people to know what they were searching for," Ryan said, regaining his casual composure with what looked like significant effort on his part.

"Or tipped off the abductor on what we were looking for," she said.

"I thought law enforcement was focused on transients."

"The sheriff's office was. Brine refused to believe someone in town could've done this. The FBI wanted to cast a wider net," Rebecca supplied, still eyeing Ryan.

"What else did they keep out of the news that might've

helped?" he asked, and she realized he was most likely just as frustrated as they were.

"That was it." Time had faded so much of her memory. The FBI had also told her that she'd been in shock, and forgetting details was her brain's natural way of protecting her. Not even a hypnotist could pull any more information out of her then. Fifteen years had surely eaten away at anything that might have been left.

With a full stomach, exhaustion set in. Her bones were so tired they ached. She leaned back against the seat, not wanting to interrupt the conversation that had turned to what each of them had been doing lately.

Brody concealed a yawn and that kicked off one for her, too.

"We should probably head back. It's an hour's drive to Mason Ridge and Rebecca hasn't slept in a day and a half," he said.

"Don't break this up because of me. It's nice to see everyone again." She couldn't remember the last time she'd sat around with friends she trusted and had a drink. College had been a blur of classes, her job as a waitress and all-night study sessions just to keep up.

Heads nodded in agreement.

"Then I think we should barbecue at the ranch next Friday night. I'll have plenty of cold beer and beds to crash on so no one has to drive," Brody said.

"I'd like to reach out to Samantha, Lisa and the others," Rebecca added. "It'll be like old times." She stopped short of saying *like when she'd been happy*.

"Until then, promise you'll get some rest. The both of you," Ryan said. "And take care of that gash on your head."

Dylan added his agreement. "We'll keep digging and

let you know if anything comes up. Forward a copy of those social-media links. Maybe I'll make a few new friends between now and then."

"Will do," Brody said.

The bill came and Dawson covered it with his hand. "I got this. You two get out of here. We'll stick around a little while and chat up the locals. See if we can dig around a little more while we're here."

Brody argued over paying the bill, lost and then thanked his friends as Rebecca hugged each one.

She wanted to talk to Ryan about his reaction earlier but tabled it. *For now.*

NIGHT HAD DESCENDED around Rebecca and Brody by the time they reached the ranch. The truck's headlights cut through the darkness, lighting a path down the drive before moving across the large ranch house as Brody pulled into his parking spot.

Rebecca tried to shake off the fog that came with drifting in and out of sleep on the way there and then waking too fast. Twelve hours underneath a warm comforter would do her good.

She blinked her eyes open and glanced at the clock. It was eleven-thirty on a Friday night. Normally, she'd be doing laundry. How lonely did that sound?

As if her past hadn't been scarring enough, the few times she'd tried to date in college hadn't worked out. One of her most distinct memories was of her first boyfriend. He'd had too much to drink one night and thought slipping her a roofie would be fun so he could "experiment." Thankfully, he'd passed out before he could do anything sick to her, but the feeling of being vulnerable had shocked her back into protective mode.

Opening up, trusting again, had been next to impossible after that. She'd met a few men in Chicago. She'd watched her drinks like a crazed person whenever she was on a date. Taking her glass of wine or cup of coffee to the bathroom with her had solicited more than a few odd looks. She didn't care. They could judge her all they wanted, but she planned to be fully alert and in control. She involuntarily shivered at the memories and the all-true thought that Brody was the only man she'd ever felt safe around. No way would he try anything funny if her back was turned. Heck, she'd kissed him twice already and he hadn't tried to push for more even though she sensed that he wanted it as much as she did.

Since moving back to Mason Ridge three years ago, the dating well had dried up.

"Hey, beautiful. You're awake." Brody's voice wrapped around her, the rich timbre sliding through her, warming her. Being near him made her want things she knew better than to consider. Things like a real man to wake up next to, to feel secure with.

He turned off the engine, cut the lights, and put his arm around her after they exited his truck.

The porch light came on unexpectedly as they approached, lighting up the front of the expansive one-story brick ranch.

Rebecca froze. "Does someone else live here with you?"

"No. It's one of those motion-sensor lights." He moved his arm from around her neck and she immediately missed the weight of it, the warmth, the feel of Brody's touch.

"You okay?"

"Yeah," she lied. How did she begin to defend just how little it took to completely rattle her nerves?

He made a move toward the front door but stopped short. Instead, he turned, captured her face in his hands and pressed his lips against hers, hard, kissing her.

She opened her mouth enough for his tongue to slip inside, where she welcomed him. The taste of sweet tea still lingered on his tongue. She tunneled her hands into his thick hair and kissed him back, matching every stroke of his tongue. And she didn't want to stop there.

He managed to pull back first. Again. "There. I've been wanting to do that again ever since we left your mother's."

She didn't immediately speak. Couldn't. Not while she could still taste him. Besides, she'd probably just say something to ruin the moment, anyway.

He mumbled an apology before sliding the key into the lock.

"Don't be sorry. I'm not."

He turned, smiled and offered his hand. She took it, electricity and awareness zinging through her. Brody was the excitement of an electrical storm blowing right through her. It was strange how safe she felt with him even though he turned everything inside her upside down.

In the porch light, she could see his face clearly. A face she'd thought about so often over the years. Remembering his features had calmed her when she woke from nightmares.

"I missed you, Brody," she said softly.

He responded by hauling her against his chest. So close, her body flush with his, she could feel his racing heartbeat against her breasts. Awareness trilled through her. She reached up on her tiptoes and wrapped her arms around his neck.

He blew out a warm breath as his hands looped around her waist. "The problem isn't how much I want you,

Rebecca. You know that, right? I'm sure sex would blow both of our minds."

This close—her breasts against his muscled chest— her nipples beaded.

"I haven't done casual sex since returning from my first tour, and I have no plans to start now. Especially not with you."

Those last words stung. She pulled back, embarrassed that she'd given in so freely to her feelings. Rather than analyzing that to death, maybe Rebecca should be relieved she felt that way at all. If Brody could unlock those feelings, then surely someone else could. "I think you misunderstood. I wasn't suggesting—"

"You might not have been, but it's been on my mind ever since I saw you this morning. And I think it's been on yours, too."

Or maybe Brody was and would always be the one she felt secure enough with to let go. And look how that had turned out, two broken hearts.

She didn't want to look into his eyes while she felt so vulnerable. He lifted her chin and that's exactly what she did—looked into those blues. Why was it the only time she felt home was when she looked at him?

Hope of another man igniting those same feelings inside her fizzled. Brody was her weakness, her hot-fudge sundae when she was supposed to be on a diet, and maybe it was time to admit he would never be more to her than a temporary treat.

"Doesn't mean we have to act on it," she said.

"Nope. Sure doesn't." He didn't immediately move.

They stood there holding each other in the moonlight, staring for long moments as though cast in stone and neither could move if they'd wanted to. She wanted to lean further into the feeling, into him, and stay there as long as she could in his arms.

"We should probably go inside," she said, losing herself in his crystalized blue gaze.

Everything about Brody reminded her of being a woman, which was something she'd neglected for so very long.

She rose up on her tiptoes and pressed a kiss to his cheek. "You've done a lot for me, Brody. More than you'll ever realize. I didn't know what to do with that when we were kids, so I pretended breaking up with you was to save you. And part of it was. The other part, the part I still don't want to admit, has to do with me. I'm trying to get over what happened, and I get close. Then, he just reaches up and takes me back down. Whether it's in a nightmare or like now, he's always going to be there, holding me back, unless I do something to change it."

His body tensed as though every muscle was fighting against the words forming in his thoughts.

"I understand," he said. "I'm sorry for what happened to you. But when this case is over, we'll go back to the way our lives were before. Yours involves taking care of your mother and working at the radio station. Mine's here on this ranch. The horses. And we need to keep that in mind before we do something that'll burn us both. No use going down that path again, wasting time."

So many objections charged through her mind, but she couldn't go there. He was right. This case would be over soon, one way or the other. That jerk would end up where he belonged, in the ground or in jail. She refused to believe he'd get to her. And they would each go back to their respective lives. Rebecca would care for her mother in her final days, and Brody would go back to his business.

And all that was going to happen whether she wanted it to or not.

She couldn't control the future. But they had now, this moment, and she didn't want it to end. She shifted her weight to the other foot, stared him directly in the eyes, and said, "I hear what you're saying and I won't argue. But I do object to one thing you said. Time spent with you is never wasted."

"I didn't mean—"

"I know exactly what you meant and I understand where you're coming from. I'm grateful for your help, so I won't push for anything else." Even though she wanted him more than she wanted to breathe. She also recognized what a huge mistake they'd be making if things went any further. As long as her mother was alive, Rebecca was tied to Mason Ridge. From the looks of her mother's condition and refusal to take medication that could save her, that wouldn't be long. Rebecca had every intention of leaving and not looking back when her mother's long battle came to an end. Whereas Brody's life was right there, doing something he loved. Everything he was building for his future was inside that county. And she admired him for knowing where his place was, where he fit. Chicago had been wonderful, mostly because it was far away from Mason Ridge. She had yet to figure out where she belonged.

Rebecca turned toward the door, easing out of Brody's grip. "I love that you bought this place. It suits you. The work that you're doing is amazing. You seem happy here."

"It's been good for me." He led her into the house and turned on the light. "No one's here and my housekeeper doesn't show up until Tuesday so we won't be bothering anyone by being here. Make all the noise you want."

The open-space living room was massive. An oversize log fireplace anchored the room on one side, and the image of a fire, glasses of wine and a bunch of throw pillows on the floor in front crossed her mind. She shook it off, instead focusing on the wood beams across the ceiling. The place was comfortable and masculine. It had that warm lodge feel to it with comfortable furniture she could sink into. Everything about the space was a true reflection of Brody. She clasped her hands together, trying to conceal her overflowing pride. Brody had done good. Better than good. "It's perfect."

His smile shouldn't make her heart flutter, and yet that's exactly what it did.

"The place has two wings, one is made up for guests and the other's mine. You can stay in the guest bedroom unless I can convince us both one night in my room would be worth it." He grinned his sexy little smile where barely the corners of his lips upturned.

She hoped he didn't notice the flush of excitement those words brought. Because right here, right now, if he seriously invited her into his bed she'd say yes.

"I'll grab a towel so you can shower." He motioned toward the long hallway to the right.

A shower sounded like heaven about now. She suppressed another yawn. "I doubt I'll be able to sleep."

"There isn't much more we can do until morning, anyway. We'll be fresh and ready to go after a good night's rest," he said.

"I don't know."

"I'll grab your suitcase, so your clothes will be waiting." He stopped long enough to give her hand a reassuring squeeze. "We'll figure this out, Rebecca."

Brody had always been able to see right through her. "I know you're right, it's just…"

"You want so badly to give your mother good news."

She nodded. "I want to give her something to fight for."

"You already have. She has you." He paused. "Besides, anything happens tonight and I promise to wake you. But you're sleepwalking at this point and you need a few hours of shut-eye before you make yourself sick."

He had a good point. And when she really thought about it, exhaustion weighed heavily on her limbs. Thoughts of a shower and sleeping in a bed were almost too good to be true. She stood and followed him down the hall. He stopped in front of a linen closet, pulled out a fresh towel and pointed toward the first door on the right.

"You'll have all the privacy you need in there."

Probably more than she wanted about then. "You going to bed, too?"

He'd already started toward the front door when he stopped and turned, sexy smile securely in place. "After a long, cold shower."

BRODY HAD BEEN awake for three hours. He'd tended to the horses, eaten breakfast and polished off a cup of coffee. He'd wanted to go inside Rebecca's room to check on her a half dozen times just to make sure she was okay but didn't. He knew better than to trust himself with her while she was vulnerable. She needed some reassurance about life, and that's most likely why she'd made it clear last night she wouldn't mind a little fooling around.

He, on the other hand, couldn't risk it. His heart couldn't take another hit.

Brody made another cup of coffee, using one of the individual cups from the single-serving machine that his housekeeper had practically forced him to buy. He settled in at the kitchen table, studying the file again. Surely something was there he could work with.

His phone vibrated. He checked the screen, found a text from Ryan wanting to know if he could stop by.

Brody responded with a yes and said the front door would be unlocked.

Ten minutes later, Ryan showed. Tension radiated from him in waves.

"That was quick." Brody glanced at the time. It was almost noon and still no sign of Rebecca.

"I was in the area," Ryan said, heading toward the kitchen. "Mind if I grab a cup of coffee and join you?"

Considering Brody lived twenty minutes from the nearest store, Ryan couldn't have been close. Brody didn't need to see the worry lines on his friend's forehead to know something was up. "You know where everything is. Make yourself at home."

"What is this? Almond mocha?" Ryan wrinkled his nose as he picked through the little pods.

"My housekeeper forced me to buy the variety pack. Said it was good to try new things. As it turns out, I'm not so much of a flavored-coffee guy. I like mine straight up and strong." Brody finished the last of his, noticing the dark circles under his buddy's eyes.

Ryan made his own cup, joined Brody at the table and took a sip.

This close, his features looked haunted. An ominous feeling settled over Brody.

"We need to talk about something Rebecca said last night. Is she up yet?" Ryan asked.

"No. She's still asleep. At least I think she is. I haven't seen her yet this morning." Brody glanced toward the guest hallway. He didn't like the way Ryan's face muscles tightened when he'd asked about Rebecca. This was disturbing.

Ryan stared into his cup for a long moment. Then, he looked up at Brody. "Are you okay?"

"You want to talk about how I'm doing?" Brody asked, surprised.

"That's not what I came here to talk about but bear with me for a sec."

Brody checked his watch. "Good. Because I have a lot to do today and I don't like where this conversation is headed."

"Fair enough," Ryan obliged. "How are you doing with all this?"

"Fine. Why? Do I seem like something's wrong?" Brody finger-combed his hair.

"Thought I picked up on something last night and you look tired this morning." Ryan shrugged.

"So I tossed and turned a little last night. I've gone days without sleep on missions. This is nothing." Brody swirled the rest of the contents in his cup. "And the reason I didn't sleep last night is because the Mason Ridge Abductor is back."

"I'm not talking about that kind of okay and you know it," Ryan said plainly.

Brody didn't immediately defend himself.

Ryan took a sip of coffee. "I'm not trying to get you riled up or dredge up the past."

"Then don't."

"It's already here. What kind of friend would I be if I didn't speak up when I thought I should?"

"I know what you're about to say and I appreciate your concern." Brody could almost hear the next words spilling out of Ryan's mouth and he hoped to preempt them.

"Because I don't think you do, I'm not going to shut up yet." Ryan gripped his mug. "Things were bad before."

"I lived it. You think I've forgotten?"

"That's not what I meant. I'm not trying to put you on the defensive. I'm offering to help. We can find a safe place for Rebecca to stay without her staying here."

"You think I can't separate my emotions long enough to take care of business?"

"I saw the way you two looked at each other last night." Ryan rubbed the day-old scruff on his chin. "Everyone noticed."

Brody had already admitted to tossing and turning all night. He'd told himself it was because of this case and not because she slept under his roof. "She was special to me a long time ago."

"And an elephant doesn't forget. Tell me something that I don't know."

"I don't feel the same way toward her anymore. Whatever we had between us died when she walked out. You know what I'm about."

"Loyalty," Ryan said without hesitation.

"Exactly. If someone can't stick with you during the tough times, then you gotta keep walking, because life is going to dish more than you can handle sometimes. Last thing I need is to be with someone I can't trust to be there when it all goes south. You know that about me." Brody's tone was a little more emphatic than he'd planned for it to be.

Ryan nodded. "Even so, there's a connection between the two of you. And that kind of link doesn't listen to reason."

Didn't Brody already know that. Last night had been a prime example of hormones trying to take control, but he'd been strong. Of course, another few seconds of her body flush with his, her heart beating against his, and he knew the story might've turned out differently. And that would've led to all kinds of awkward today. He didn't want to think about what might've happened if he hadn't practiced restraint. He didn't want to talk about this. He wanted to focus on the case. And he knew Ryan had shown up to discuss more than just *this*. Brody figured he needed to throw his friend a bone. "I'd be lying if I denied having feelings for her. Believe me when I say that I know what's good for me in the long run. And the woman sleeping in the other room is not it."

He pointed toward the hallway where she slept and his gaze followed.

She was standing there, chin up, defiance in her stare. The exact look she gave when the pain was more than she could process.

Damn. Damn. Damn.

A few other choice words flashed through his mind. Brody hadn't meant for her to hear what he was saying. Truth was that he didn't know exactly how he felt about her. Yes, he had feelings. Yes, they were strong. Yes, he wanted to take her to bed more than he wanted air. But he had to consider the possibility that this need could be nothing more than residual hurt from a wounded teenager. He'd been destroyed when she'd broken it off with him.

At eighteen, he couldn't think of a future without her. His plans to go into the military, to come back and buy the ranch, all of this, had been to create a life for her. He could see the fault in that plan now. Both parties needed to be on board. He had never shared his ideas with her. And he was still asking himself why he'd returned to Mason Ridge when those plans had been blown to high heaven. He told himself that it was to be close to his father, but

Brody could've gone anywhere after the military. When the time came and his father couldn't take care of himself, Brody doubted it would matter where they'd settled.

Rebecca had wanted to be out of Mason Ridge as soon as she came of age. She'd said that she'd broken up with him to save him from himself. Had it really been to free herself so she could get out of this town and not look back just like his mother?

Plus, it wasn't like she'd come back for him. She hadn't reached out once since she'd gone. The only reason she was here now was to be near her ailing mother in her final months. Mrs. Hughes looked to be barely hanging on. As soon as death took her, Rebecca would disappear again. Just like his mother. And there Brody was, just like his father, waiting for a woman who could walk away so easily.

There was no denying that Brody and Rebecca shared feelings. There'd be no point fighting the fact that those feelings, whatever else they were, were strong. But it was probably just unfinished business between them. And even if it wasn't, no good could come from acting on it. Period.

Rebecca hadn't even stuck around for graduation. The last day of school, she'd gone home, packed her bags and caught a flight north to go to school.

Brody knew because he'd stopped by, lovesick, about to ship out but unable to go without seeing her one more time, without being sure that's what she wanted.

She was long gone. No goodbyes.

It had hardened Brody in a good way. Made him suck it up and endure basic training. Falling into his bunk every night exhausted had been a welcome relief to the living hell of realizing the one person who was everything good in your life didn't blink an eye about boarding a plane without a backward glance.

In some ways, he owed his elite status to her. It was because of Rebecca he'd worked his tail off, preferring to punish himself day after day in training so he could fall into bed numb every night. She was the reason he'd maintained focus when others couldn't wait for leave to see their loved ones. Because of Rebecca, he'd kept everyone but his father at a safe distance ever since.

No distractions.

And all those feelings dissolved as she stood there for a long moment, in the hallway, not speaking. Brody's oversize T-shirt long enough to hit midthigh. Then she said, "That one of those pod coffeemakers?"

Ryan's gaze bounced between Brody and Rebecca, stopping long enough to relay an unspoken apology to both. "I better head home. There's something else I'd like to discuss with you, Brody. I'll give you a call later."

"No, please don't leave because of me," Rebecca said, crossing over to the kitchen. "I'll join you both for a cup of coffee."

Ryan nodded.

She made a cup and took a seat at the table, pulling the shirt over her knees as she hugged them into her chest. "What's the plan for today?"

Ryan stared into his cup again for a long moment.

Tension was like a wall between them.

"You said something last night that I can't get out of my mind." His jaw clenched as he looked up at Rebecca.

The knowing look she gave Ryan when she nodded had Brody almost thinking she'd been expecting this conversation. What had he missed that she'd picked up on?

"You mentioned apple tobacco. I didn't know about

that before." Ryan paused, his gaze returned to the cup. "Before I say anything else, I just want to say that I'm sure my brother wasn't involved. I know him."

"What exactly are you saying, Ryan?" Brody asked.

Rebecca didn't budge and she looked small, sitting there. Brody fisted his hands to stop them from reaching for her.

"My brother came home smelling like that sometimes. I'd know that scent anywhere, Rebecca. The one you're talking about is distinct."

"I know it wasn't your brother, Ryan," Rebecca said reassuringly. "It couldn't be him. Your brother's tall and stocky like you. You guys have a football build whereas this guy is tall and slim. Plus, I think he's older than Justin."

Ryan didn't look relieved. "He'd smoke it with my uncle when they'd get drunk together back in Justin's troubled days. So, I lay awake last night asking myself if Justin didn't have anything to do with this, and I know in my heart he didn't, then who could it be? What are the chances a transient smokes apple tobacco. It's not exactly a common thing. If we stop looking at random people who could've been in town for the festival and set our sights on people right here, then that changes everything. And right now the evidence points to my uncle."

"What's his build?" Brody asked.

"He's tall and thin."

Chapter Nine

Rebecca touched Ryan's hand to comfort him. "Doesn't mean it was him."

"I hope not. But I gotta look at the facts and be honest with myself, with you," Ryan said, his anguish written all over his face. "He's been in trouble with the law, but I can't believe he would do something like this."

"We can see if he was a suspect." Brody studied the police file.

"Do you know where he lives? We can go talk to him," Rebecca offered.

"I haven't seen him in a while. Last I knew he was living in Garland."

"That's half an hour away from Mason Ridge at the most," Brody said. He stopped suddenly.

Rebecca didn't like his expression. But then, she was still reeling from Brody's words while she'd stood in the hallway. They stung, even though she knew he was just speaking the truth. Stuffing those feelings down deep, she took another sip of coffee.

"Turns out, your uncle Gregory was a suspect," Brody said, flashing an apologetic look toward Ryan. "He worked as a delivery driver for a Texas nursery chain around the time of the abductions."

"Which would put him on the highways," Rebecca said.

"The sheriff would've been able to match up his delivery schedule," Brody said quietly. He kept skimming the file.

"My uncle did stupid things when he drank, but he wasn't violent."

"There isn't much more in the file that I can see. Think we can speak to him?" Brody asked.

"No other kids have gone missing in the area since Shane. If his uncle was somehow involved, wouldn't there be others?" Rebecca asked.

"The Glenn boy last year in Sunnyvale," Brody reminded her.

"True." She nodded.

"I thought about that, too. My uncle moved to Garland two years after the disappearance," Ryan said. "Last time I saw him a few years ago his hands shook if he didn't have a drink by ten o'clock in the morning. He's done other stupid stuff, illegal. Been in jail a couple of times. My heart doesn't want to believe he's capable of such a heinous act and yet I can't ignore the facts. What if he did this?"

"I hear what you're saying. It's probably not even him, but it's smart to check into every possibility. I appreciate you coming forward. This must be really hard for you," Rebecca said. A man who couldn't go a day without drinking most likely wouldn't have the strength to subdue both her and Shane, could he? There was another way to solve this. She remembered that her attacker had spoken the other morning in the parking lot. If it had been Ryan's uncle, she would be able to recognize his voice. "I might have a way to resolve this. Does your uncle have a phone?"

"I believe so. Why?"

Brody was already nodding. He'd caught on to what she wanted to do.

"Call him and put it on speaker."

"Justin might have the number." Ryan pulled out his cell. After a quick call to his brother, he punched in the digits. The line rang three times before rolling into voice mail. Ryan's thumb moved over to end the call.

"Don't hang up. Hold on a second before you do that," Rebecca said, stopping him.

This is Greg. You know what to do at the beep.

Brody's gaze was intent on her, studying her.

"Doesn't sound like him," Rebecca said on a sigh of relief. She wanted to find Shane's abductor more than anything but not at the cost of one of her friends. "At least I don't think."

"We can't ignore the possibility that he might know something or be connected in some way," Brody said, looking to Ryan. "Does your uncle have any enemies?"

"My first thought would be Alcorn. He hates all of my family members. You think someone else might try to set him up?" Ryan asked, his voice hopeful. He deflated a second later. "Why would someone do that after all these years? And why to him? It's not like he's rich or power-ful. There's nothing to blackmail him for. Even Alcorn has given up."

"The word about apple tobacco might have gotten out. This is a small town, and after running into Peter Shef-field last night I started thinking how hard it can be to keep secrets. All it would take is one leak. Someone had to have seen something."

"I'd like to chat with your uncle," Brody said.

"I'll arrange something and get back to you." Ryan's face muscles were tight.

Brody checked his phone. "I just got a text from Samantha. She's trying to pull together the other girls to swing by tomorrow afternoon. She's already in town to see her father, anyway."

Samantha had moved to Dallas after college for a job in the textile industry.

The reunion with the guys had gone well, so Rebecca was hopeful this would, too. Was it possible to pick up friendships after everything that had happened? Rebecca hoped so. It was a nice feeling to be with people she had so much history with. They were the few people who didn't look at her awkwardly anymore, as if seeing her reminded them horrible things could happen at any moment. "I can't wait to see her and the others. It's been such a long time. In the meantime, we'll keep following leads, right?"

"The festival rolls up the tents tomorrow. I'd initially hoped to wait and see if things calmed down after they leave. But then I checked online this morning and the Glenns' son, Jason, who disappeared in Sunnyvale last year, did so while the festival was packing up," Brody said.

Ryan perked up. "That's a strange coincidence."

"I'm not so sure that timing is accidental," Brody agreed. "Who's in charge of the festival?"

"Charles Alcorn heads it up every year," Ryan supplied.

"Isn't the festival too low-brow for him to be involved?" Brody asked.

"You'd think so," Ryan said. "But they use his land and he makes a fortune every year."

"I wonder if we can get a list of vendors from him? Names?" Brody asked.

"Doesn't hurt to ask," Rebecca said with a quick look toward Brody.

"He has offices downtown in the building next to the mayor's office, doesn't he?" Brody asked with a slight nod.

"He does. Nice building. I saw in a magazine that he renovated the whole inside before moving in a couple of years ago. Only the finest quality furniture. The best finishings. He donated the other half of the building to the city."

"How convenient for him to be right next door to the mayor."

"Easier to line Mayor Garza's pockets when he only has to walk four steps," Rebecca said. It was common knowledge he had a do-what-it-takes-to-get-the-job-done philosophy. It was half the reason she was tempted to take him up on his offer of help.

"In the meantime, we'll keep poking around until we figure this out." Ryan pushed his chair back from the table. "I have a few things to take care of. Keep me posted on what you find out. I'll let you know as soon as I arrange a meeting with my uncle. Stay close to your phone."

"Will do," Brody said, turning to Rebecca as soon as the door was closed.

"You noticed that, too, didn't you?" she asked.

"Yep. Ryan sure got out of here quick when we started talking about Alcorn." Brody stood, walked to the sink and rinsed out his coffee cup. "There's no love lost between their families. Ryan's dad wouldn't give Alcorn something he wanted years and years ago when he was still alive."

"That wouldn't have gone over well. Guess I wasn't

around much to notice." She'd been so wrapped up in her own family's issues she hadn't once stopped to consider her friends' problems. "I remember bad blood from when we were kids now that I think about it."

Brody crossed to the back door. "Some old wounds don't heal."

BRODY EXERCISED THE HORSES, taking care not to overtax his newest arrival, Storm Rival. The owner didn't have any use for the chestnut Thoroughbred when he developed shin splints after his last race at Lone Star Park. Brody just called him Red. Red had been a promising two-year-old until this happened. Now his future was uncertain. He had a true splint, the worst-case scenario for a racehorse, as evidenced by the bulge just below his left knee and on the inner side of his leg. The problem was all too common in young horses entering heavy training. Bad cases had ended plenty of promising careers.

His owner had been kind and this guy was going to get a second chance in life, a different life. The hefty donation would help keep things running, too.

Being in the barn, away from Rebecca, was a good thing. Her lips were too full, too pink, too damn tempting.

Work was the best distraction.

After he'd arranged care for the evening, he cut across the yard and back to the house.

Rebecca was still at the table, studying the screen on Brody's laptop.

On Brody's phone was a text from Ryan. "Ryan may have found something interesting and he wants us to come check it out. He isn't far from here. Are you good with that?"

Rebecca nodded.

"We can be out of here in fifteen minutes. I just need to get dressed," she said, disappearing down the hall.

Brody forced his gaze away from her backside. Self-discipline was the biggest difference between a man and a boy. While he waited, he took pictures of the suspect list so he'd have it with him in case they came across a name.

She returned ten minutes later, fresh-faced, hair pulled back in a ponytail. Her jeans, low on her hips, fit her curves to perfection. The material of her light blue blouse was just thin enough to allow a peek at her matching lacy bra. "Ready?"

For more than she knew. "Yep."

"I checked the news while you were taking care of the horses." Rebecca moved to the driver's side.

"I'm okay to drive."

She gave him the look that he knew better than to argue with, so he didn't. He held his hands up in surrender. "Okay. Fine."

Taking control behind the wheel, she held out his keys. "Didn't figure you'd get far without these, anyway. And your head is still healing."

"I've taken worse blows than that and survived." To his ego, for one.

"Can you give me directions? His position should be on your phone, right?"

Brody pulled up Ryan's location using the GPS tracker on his phone. He raised the volume and set the phone between them on the seat.

She cranked the ignition and backed out of the parking spot. "This has all been so crazy I don't think I stopped to thank you for what you did for my mother yesterday afternoon."

"Not a problem," he said casually, and meant it.

"I'm serious. She can be difficult to deal with and I think she was shocked to see you."

"Nah. She was fine. Plus, there was a lot going on. Under the circumstances, I thought she was rather nice."

"And if I admit to being wrong about something, will you promise not to rub it in?" she asked.

"Depends on what it is."

She stopped at the end of the drive long enough to jab his arm. "Be serious."

"I am. Scout's honor."

"Like you were a Boy Scout." She rolled her eyes and made a right turn toward town. "Fine, then I won't tell you."

"Oh, come on. You know I was just kidding." He used to love making her laugh in high school. Her smiles were rare, laughter even more so, and he figured that made them all the more special.

"So you think I'm going to tell you now that you've done a little begging?" She didn't hold back her laugh.

"Any chance it's working?"

"Okay, fine. What's it going to cost me?" He paused long enough to listen to the next instruction from the GPS.

She turned right, as instructed, then nodded. Her serious expression returned.

"You plan to tell me, or did you bring it up just to torture me?" he asked, trying to bring the lighter Rebecca back to life. She was inside there. He knew it and he wanted more of her.

"Fine. I lied to you before to trick you into seeing my mother. You were right. She didn't like you." She cracked a shy smile.

"I believe I won her over."

"Agreed. I wasn't sure what to expect, but you broke through to her." She paused. "I feel so bad for the Glenns."

"They've been through the ringer. It's obvious on their faces."

Again, she nodded.

"You rarely ever talk about Shane. Is that subject off-limits?"

Rebecca neither spoke nor nodded.

"You don't have to now. I just thought maybe it might help or some—"

"Don't feel bad about asking, Brody."

"I don't," he reassured, but she was dead-on. He felt bad for bringing up Shane.

"I should talk about him more. About what happened. Maybe it'll help us figure things out. You say we're down to a couple dozen names aside from Ryan's uncle, right?" She paused long enough to receive and follow GPS directions.

She didn't need to tell him about her pain. He felt it, based on the heaviness in her words, the determination in her features.

Brody leaned forward in his seat and stretched his arms.

"All I can really remember about my brother came from stories from my mom and pictures she showed. Other than that night, of course. I can't seem to forget that. All I keep thinking is who would do something like this to an innocent boy? I mean, the guy has to be a monster, right?" Rebecca's body shuddered just talking about it. "Or, maybe he's crazy."

"You won't get an argument out of me that the man's crazy or needs to be locked up with the key tossed away for good. Hell, give me five minutes alone with him and the bastard won't hurt another child for the rest of his life."

The GPS interrupted, stating that the destination was two blocks up on the right. The distraction gave Brody a minute to regroup as Rebecca drove to the spot and then pulled into a parking space.

"Odd. I expected to see Ryan's SUV here," he said.

"I did, too," Rebecca agreed.

"Something doesn't feel right about this." Brody surveyed the area. He phoned Ryan, but he didn't pick up. "I think you should let me drop you off in town so I can investigate."

"And leave you alone with those bumps and bruises? Not a chance."

"I'm better today. I'll grab Dylan or Dawson. It's the weekend. One of them should be around. On second thought, I'll call Dawson. Dylan will be with his little girl today." He prepared himself for a fight.

"Take me to Angel's. That way, when you come to pick me up, we'll be able to get a decent piece of pie," Rebecca said.

Grateful she didn't put up an argument, he palmed his cell and fired off a text to Samantha. He had no plans to leave Rebecca alone. "Mind if I arrange a little company for you? I don't want you to sit there by yourself going crazy worrying until I get back."

"What makes you think I'll do that?"

"Because I've met you before, remember? It's me, Brody."

"Okay, funny man." She paused, looking resigned. "But you're probably right. Samantha did say she'd be in town this weekend. Maybe we'll get lucky and she'll be available. It would be nice to see her."

Lucky. There was that word again. "Done. She just texted back to say she'd meet us there in fifteen. Okay if she brings her father?"

"All right by me."

The extra fifteen minutes it took to drop Rebecca off at Angel's had Brody's gut tied in knots. He sure as hell hoped Ryan wasn't lying in the woods somewhere, helpless. The image didn't do good things to Brody's blood pressure. He phoned his friend again. Same result.

Bringing Rebecca into those same woods where they'd been attacked felt all kinds of wrong. No way could he take a chance with her safety. And he had the very real feeling they could've been lured into a trap.

REBECCA HAD DOWNED another full cup of coffee and was feeling much more awake and alert by the time Samantha arrived with her father. Mr. Turner had aged quite a bit since Rebecca had last seen him. His entire head was covered in white and his frame was thinning. The hardware store he owned in town most likely still kept him in shape.

Throwing her arms up, Rebecca waved at the pair. She was greeted with a huge smile from Samantha, but Mr. Turner hesitated. He said something to his daughter, but they were too far away for Rebecca to make it out.

When Samantha pointed at Rebecca and nodded, Mr. Turner looked downright uncomfortable. Not an unusual reaction from people in town, but it reminded Rebecca just what an outcast she was in her own hometown. And as much as she'd love to keep her mother around for many more years, healthy, Rebecca was eager to move back to a bigger town. Chicago had been kind to her. And best of all, no one knew about her past there. She didn't get those same wide-eyed stares and behind-the-back whispers when people passed by her in the streets as she did in Mason Ridge. Don't get her wrong, she loved her hometown more than anything, just not some of the baggage that came with it.

Samantha led her reluctant father to the table and plopped down. He did not. "It's so good to see you, Rebecca. You remember my father."

"Of course. Mr. Turner, it's so nice to see you again." With her mother in long-term care and Rebecca herself living in a rental, she hadn't had much need to stop by the hardware store. She stood and stuck out her hand.

He obliged, shaking just long enough to be polite.

Rebecca noticed his palm was warm, sweaty. Since when did her presence start making people so nervous? She was used to seeing sadness in everyone's eyes. Some were upset even and she figured they didn't want to be reminded of that summer. But nervous? She'd moved into a whole new category. *Great.*

Maybe she had always made people feel that way and she'd been too trapped inside her own head to notice.

"I'm sorry I can't join you two," he started.

"Daddy saw some friends at the counter. He asked if we'd mind if he ate lunch with them."

"Not at all," Rebecca said, figuring he didn't look too sorry. In fact, he looked like he might jump out of his skin if she said, "Boo!"

He scurried off to join a couple of older men seated at the bar stools at the breakfast counter.

When he was out of earshot Samantha leaned in, embarrassment flushing her cheeks, and said, "Honestly, I don't know what's wrong with him lately. Getting old, I guess."

Rebecca figured she had a good handle on his sudden

need to eat lunch with someone else, anyone else. The man looked like he'd seen a ghost, which was par for the course for her and another reason she didn't mind working the graveyard shift. She figured most parents didn't want to be reminded what could've happened to their child instead of Shane. "It's fine. This will give us a chance to really talk. We'd bore him to death with our conversation, anyway."

Samantha flashed a grateful look and then summoned the waiter. "I swear he's starting to get senile. And the man doesn't sit still anymore."

"He's fine. Don't worry about it."

The waiter interrupted their conversation. Samantha ordered a club sandwich and sweet tea.

"I should have a salad, but I can't resist the burgers here," Rebecca confessed. "Looks like I'll be hitting the gym later."

"It's so good to see you. How long has it been?"

Rebecca didn't want to try to reach back too far. "I know I haven't seen you since we headed to different colleges."

"Our ten-year reunion is like next year." Samantha's look of horror brought a smile to Rebecca's face.

"Already? Man, time flies."

"I somehow got hooked with planning duties. I'm on the attendance committee, which basically means I'm responsible for finding everyone and making sure they show up."

Rebecca gave a full-body shiver. "Count me out."

"You have to come. If only to support me," Samantha said on a laugh.

"Do you stay in touch with Lisa or Melanie?"

"Mostly just Melanie. She moved to Houston after

college so we don't get to see each other as much as we'd like. Lisa's not too far, though. I've run into her a few times at the grocery with Pops. I meant to call her today."

"I'd love to see both of them again. I work deep nights, so even though I live nearby I never see anyone." She decided not to share just how on purpose that was. But seeing Samantha was nice. Rebecca hadn't realized just how much she'd missed having this kind of friendship. Ties that ran deep.

"Melanie never comes back." Samantha rolled her eyes. "Says her work keeps her too busy and she doesn't get a lot of vacation time. When she does, she likes to see someplace new."

That last bit of information came out a little too quickly. Samantha practically stumbled over the words in her rush to explain.

Rebecca had no intention of making anyone else uncomfortable, not on purpose. Most people didn't want anything to do with her anymore and she understood on some level. They couldn't help, so they'd wanted to forget. She was just a big old fat reminder of the worst summer in the history of Mason Ridge, of every parent's worst nightmare. Plus, everyone had known and loved Shane. She couldn't blame them for not wanting to be reminded of the horrible incident that took him away from them. If it hadn't happened to her family, she might be able to look the other way, too.

"Okay, you got me. I'll come to the reunion," Rebecca said, mostly to redirect the conversation.

"Seriously? You will?" Again, her friend looked grateful for the change of subject.

"If I'm in town." She wanted to add, *and still alive.*

Chapter Ten

Brody picked Dawson up at their meeting point on his way to find Ryan, regretting the extra five minutes it took.

"Have you heard from Ryan at all today?" Brody asked, checking his phone again after pulling into the spot he and Rebecca had occupied nearly half an hour ago. He'd brought his friend up-to-date on the short ride over.

"Nope. Not a word. But then that's not unusual," Dawson said, shoving the last bite of a burrito into his mouth.

Having along a guy as big as Dawson, with almost twice Brody's strength, was a good thing, Brody figured.

"Let's see if we can figure out what's going on." Brody didn't like how Ryan had looked earlier. The edge to his tone hadn't sat well with Brody. After the revelation about Ryan's uncle, he looked even more determined to figure out what was going on. Brody sent another text to Ryan and then waited.

There was no response. Again.

"Here's the most logical place to park, but Ryan's vehicle is nowhere." Brody checked the navigation system's map. If he could believe what was on the screen then Ryan was fifty feet or so off the road.

He and Dawson got out of his truck and headed toward the dot on the screen. As they moved, he thought about the missing Sunnyvale boy, the timing. There had to be a connection. What were they missing? But then, getting inside the head of a man who'd abducted a child wouldn't be easy. What about the age of the Glenn kid? He was seven just as Shane had been. Were there other cases in Texas of seven-year-olds going missing? Did the abductor live in Texas? Brody had to think so.

This far, they didn't have squat to go on except a vague description. The hoodie and sunglasses blocked his face and Rebecca had not been able to get a good view of the guy during either encounter, which was frustrating. No more so than the blow to Brody's head. Having his skull traumatized didn't make for the best recall. Brody made a mental note to run a search for crimes connected to seven-year-old boys in Texas.

The phone vibrated. Brody checked the screen. He had another email from the feed store. Still no word from Ryan.

Cell coverage would become spotty the closer he moved into Woodrain Park. On the other hand, the fact he hadn't heard from Rebecca was good news. Even so, a bad feeling crept up his spine. Call it instinct, intuition or a sixth sense, Brody didn't care. Whatever it was had kept him alive in more than one dicey situation in the military.

For Ryan's sake, Brody hoped like hell Greg hadn't been involved. Brody vaguely remembered the guy hanging around Ryan's house in the summers. Even then Brody knew the guy was no good. Did that mean he was a kidnapper? A murderer?

Rebecca had dismissed it, but Brody couldn't stop thinking about the apple tobacco. What was the chance that was a coincidence?

"I know this area," Dawson said. "These woods connect to Mason Ridge Lake on the south side."

"Which means the RV park where most of the festival workers stay is just on the other side of the lake," Brody agreed, now that he was getting his bearings. The workers pretty much stuck to themselves when they came through town, unlike the winter carnival crew, who would show up in restaurants, chat up locals and walk the town square. The only times he remembered seeing festival people were early in the mornings at the grocery when he'd had occasion to go. And, sometimes, late nights at the Laundromat, although they hung most of their clothes to dry near the lake. If one of their machines needed a part, they'd show up at the hardware store, but that was a rare sighting. The nearest auto shop was in Sunnyvale. If one of their vehicles had trouble, they'd have to go there or be towed. Brody hadn't thought much about their habits before.

Being a Renaissance Festival, people walked around in sixteenth-century costumes. There were horse games played and turkey legs for sale. The workers kept to themselves. He figured the lack of workers in town had more to do with them sleeping in mornings and the fact there wasn't much to do in Mason Ridge.

Dawson followed closely behind as Brody led the way through the thicket.

The lake was coming into view by the time they reached the spot where Ryan should be. "This is it."

"He has to be around here somewhere." The day was in full swing and Brody could see festival workers from across the lake. They looked to be gathered in a circle. Were they having a meeting? "What's going on over there?"

"Hard to tell from here." He moved out of the tree

line and to the water's edge. "It looks like they're sitting around having lunch."

Brody moved next to him. Kids ran around, kicking and chasing a ball. A woman was hanging clothes on the line she'd set up from a lamppost to her RV. Nothing suspicious appeared to be going on. It all looked like pretty normal stuff to Brody.

A text came through. Brody checked his phone. It was from Ryan. "He wants to meet at the picnic tables." Branches broke to their left.

Brody whirled around. The trees were thick enough to block his view. He locked gazes with Dawson and then motioned for him to break to the left. Brody broke to the right, his steps so light they made no sound. Dawson's hunting instincts must've kicked in, because he didn't make a noise, either.

The sound Brody heard might have been an animal and that was the most logical answer. No one, and especially not the Mason Ridge Abductor, would be dumb enough to attack them in broad daylight. Then again, he'd just tried that with Rebecca.

Let him pick on someone his own size, Brody thought, stepping ever so softly through the underbrush.

He and Dawson would come at whomever or whatever was making the noise from opposite sides. It was the best way to surprise him.

Another noise sounded, indicating more movement. Brody tracked farther to the left, hoping Dawson was correcting his position as well and that he wasn't being lured into a trap. This scenario had stink bait written all over it.

What if it was Ryan?

Brody reminded himself that cell coverage was spotty in the woods. Or...

A bad thought hit Brody. Ryan would answer his phone if he *could*.

Whatever was making that sound was on the move. And that had to be a good thing, because if it was Ryan that meant he was capable of walking.

Brody picked up a rock the size of his fist and hurled it toward a tree ten feet away to see if he could stir up more movement. An animal would react instantly to the sound and scatter.

He stilled.

Sounds of children's laughter floated across the lake. No bolt from an animal.

Meaning the noise was being made by a person.

A muttered curse followed a grunt and a thud. Then a call for help shot through the trees. Dawson.

Brody broke into a run toward the sound, branches slapping him in the face and underbrush stabbing needles in his shoes.

A large man was hovering over Dawson, who was on his side on the ground. Brody dove straight into the guy, knocking him off balance.

Dawson immediately rolled away and then jumped to his feet. He moved so quickly the guy didn't have time to react. Brody had already pinned the guy with his thighs. "You like sneaking up on people in the woods?"

"I was just thinking the same thing about you," the guy ground out. "What are you doing over here, sneaking around, watching my friends?"

Hope that this could be The Mason Ridge Abductor died instantly based on this guy's size and general stature. He was big and powerful. Not thin, like Rebecca had said.

"We're looking for our friend."

"Get off me and I'll help."

Brody nodded to Dawson, who eased off the festival worker. He was a big guy with a ponytail. He was a bit older, his white hair streaked with gray.

"If your friends are over there, then what are you doing sneaking around on this side of the lake?" Brody asked.

The man dusted the dirt off his jeans and then took the hand up Brody offered. "My name's Lester Simmons."

"We heard a woman was attacked at the grocery nearby and we didn't want to take any chances. We travel with our wives and children to a different city every week. We've seen and heard just about everything. No one wanted to risk it so we set up watch," Lester said. His deep-set brown eyes and permanent smile lines softened what could have been an intimidating figure. One phone call and he could have a dozen men bolting around that lake. The tables would be turned. Brody and Dawson would be completely outnumbered.

Brody gave a nod of understanding and provided a description of Ryan. "According to GPS on his phone, he should be in this area."

"Hold on." Lester pulled his cell from his back pocket.

"Whoa. Not so fast."

"I already have guys on their way. I'm not dumb enough to investigate a sound alone. Figure I'll give them a heads-up so they can look for your friend." Lester went to work on his phone.

"Thank you," Brody said. "Sorry about before."

"It's cool. Tensions are high around camp, too." Lester pocketed his phone. "Where'd you leave off?"

"The last message I received from him said he'd be near the picnic tables," Brody said, remembering the area.

"There's a set right over here. We come over sometimes

for dinner because the barbecue grills are less crowded on this side." Lester led them to the tree line."

Sure enough there was a set of picnic tables nestled near a cove. No sign of Ryan.

None of this made sense.

Brody fired off another text to his friend and moved to the location Ryan said he'd be.

No response. No luck.

More men arrived, coming from every direction, and offered the same response when asked if they'd seen anyone else.

The area had been thoroughly searched and there was still no word from or sign of Ryan. It wasn't like him to pull a prank or do something like this. Brody didn't like it one bit.

"Think we should check his place?" Dawson asked. "Maybe he gave up waiting and headed home."

"That's a good idea. There's no sign of him here and we've been searching for more than an hour." Brody had an idea. He called Ryan's phone and then listened. The buzzing sound came a few seconds later. Brody moved to it, located the device.

"Looks like he was here. I'll take this back to him." Brody swiped his finger across the screen. Sure enough, the texts were there. He scanned the log for any others that might give a clue as to where Ryan could be. There was nothing. Brody turned to Lester. "Your help is much appreciated. I apologize again for the misunderstanding earlier."

Lester's friends looked over at him in confusion.

"Not a problem. Like I said, everyone's on alert around here." Lester smiled and took the hand being offered in a hearty shake.

On the way back to the truck, Brody filled Dawson in on the phone's contents. Dawson double-checked the logs and didn't find anything that stood out, either.

At least they'd made a contact within the festival ranks. Having an ally there might come in handy later. There were so many of them around town for the festival, which wrapped up tomorrow. The more eyes and ears, the better. And it was also helpful to know his family and friends were as concerned as the rest of the town.

Turns out, the festival crowd wasn't so different from the people of Mason Ridge.

Finding Ryan had just become top priority.

The drive to his house took another twenty minutes. Brody parked across the street and then texted Rebecca to find out if she was doing okay.

Rebecca replied that she and Samantha were catching up and he could take his time getting back to the restaurant.

As Brody opened the door to get out, his phone rang. The name of the caller was Rebecca.

Odd.

He quickly answered.

"Brody, I thought you'd want to know that Ryan just walked in."

"He's okay?"

"Not a scratch on him," she replied matter-of-factly.

"Hold on to him for me, okay?" Brody stopped Dawson and ended the call. "False alarm. He just showed up at Angel's in town."

"That's strange."

"Isn't it? At least we know he's not lying in a ditch somewhere." Relief settled over Brody and he realized how clenched his shoulder muscles had been. "Want me to drop you off at your house?"

Dawson nodded as he got back in the truck. "It's been a crazy few days, hasn't it?"

It was more statement than question.

"Sure has." Brody gripped the steering wheel tighter, readying himself for more warnings about his relationship with Rebecca.

"You have everything covered out at the ranch?"

"Thanks for the other day. My neighbor helped out last night and my part-time help pulled an extra shift this morning. So far, so good."

"Call me if you need more help."

"Will do."

Brody shot Dawson a look.

"What?" Dawson asked.

"Nothing. I just thought you were going to warn me about spending time with Rebecca," Brody said, easing his grip on the wheel.

"Sounds like something Ryan would do."

"He already did."

"Then you don't need to hear it from me."

"No. I don't."

"Besides, I got a different opinion about that, anyway." Dawson chuckled. "And you know what they say about opinions and how much they stink."

"I sure do," Brody agreed. "I'd like to hear what you have to say, anyway."

"The two of you together is a good thing in my book. It's natural."

"Us being together has never been the tricky part. It's when she leaves that does me in."

Dawson nodded. "I get that."

"The last time wasn't exactly a trip to the state fair."

"I remember. You were a mess."

"Thanks," Brody said sarcastically.

"Anytime," Dawson shot back, clearly trying to work off the tension they'd both felt. "How do you know she'll do it again? I mean, give her some credit. She's a grown woman now, not some young kid scared of her own shadow."

"True," Brody agreed. "In my experience, when people tell you who they are, it's smart to believe them."

"And actions speak louder than words."

"Most clichés are rooted in truth. That's why they're repeated over and over again."

"Except that she's not the same person she was before. Not in my opinion. And I don't remember her making any promises she'd stick around before."

"Tell that to a kid. Here's another problem you might not have considered." Brody pulled up in front of their meeting place. He lived a few towns over. "Don't both parties have to want to be in a relationship for it to work?"

The door was open and Dawson was half-out when he turned. "Had your eyes checked lately? Because I'm starting to think you're going blind."

Was his vision impaired when it came to Rebecca? He felt the heat between them—there was no questioning their attraction. Could there be more?

It took more than good chemistry to make a relationship work.

Dawson held on to the door. "You remember to call me if you need a hand around the ranch. You hear?"

"I plan to take you up on that offer. And thank you."

"Good. Consider the other stuff I said, too."

"You bet." Brody obliged his friend and appreciated

his point of view. Ultimately, relationships came down to loyalty.

And he was grateful for Dawson's.

REBECCA DIDN'T REALIZE that she'd been in the booth for almost three hours by the time Brody walked through the door of Angel's. She waved him over, thinking how fast time had zipped by.

By the second hour, Mr. Turner had excused himself, telling Samantha he could walk home from the restaurant.

Of course, she'd tried to talk him out of going. He'd told her that he wanted to stop by some of the shops in the square, anyway.

Reluctantly, Samantha had let him go. She'd mumbled another apology, which was unnecessary, and had said that he never got over the abductions. He'd said that he wished he could help in some way but had felt as helpless then as he did now. Some people got over the past better than others. Since Rebecca and Samantha had been friends all those years ago, the whole ordeal most likely hit a little too close to home for Mr. Turner. With the loss of his wife the previous year, it might've been too much for him.

Rebecca understood and had assured her friend there was no harm done.

Those thoughts washed away as Brody opened the door and made a straight line to Rebecca. His head was down, but his gaze was intense and a little part of her wondered if he'd missed her, too.

Ryan, who had been seated next to her, stood as Brody approached the table. The two shook hands and then he leaned over to hug Samantha.

When Ryan sat down again, he moved across the table, leaving the spot next to Rebecca free.

"My phone's missing," he repeated, this time saying it to Brody.

"When did you notice it was gone?"

"Not until she asked me about the text message I sent." He motioned toward Rebecca. "Thing is, I didn't send it."

"You couldn't have," Brody said.

Chapter Eleven

Brody held out Ryan's phone. "There were all kinds of festival people in the area where someone told us to meet. They were trading watch."

"One of them must've lifted my phone at the gas station earlier when I stopped to get gas. I keep it in my pocket and hardly think about it until I need it. I've never been one of those people glued to the screen." Ryan took the offering. He should look relieved that his uncle might be innocent. Instead, he looked even more worried. "You think one of them tried to isolate you? Get you in the woods?"

"Makes me think someone's watching. Whoever's behind this is most likely still trying to get to Rebecca. But now I may have a contact inside the Renaissance camp." Of course, the guy could have been covering for one of his own. "I met a guy named Lester. He seemed like a good person albeit protective of his people. We might be able to get more information from him."

"We still need to circle back and talk to Uncle Greg," Ryan said.

Brody's coffee arrived.

"I stopped by Alcorn's office and caught a break when his admin was there working. I wasn't sure she would be given this is Saturday. I used Rebecca's name. She turned over a list of vendor names. We can check them against the suspect list to see how many hits we get. We'll focus on those first." Sitting so close to Rebecca had Brody's pulse racing again.

"I think we should speak to my uncle first," Ryan said.

"We can always drive to Garland and check his last-known address," Brody offered.

Rebecca touched his arm. He ignored the heat exploding through him. Everything inside him wanted to haul her in his arms. He picked up his coffee instead of reaching for her. This seemed a good time to remind himself of the fact that most high school sweethearts who went on to marry didn't make it to their third anniversary, or so he'd been told. He already knew how much it hurt when a relationship didn't work. His friends had offered all kinds of unsolicited advice and encouragement when she'd walked out before.

Dismissing the notion of him and Rebecca still together before it could gain traction and make him miss something he shouldn't want he said, "Ryan, you could drive."

"Or we could go back and rest first. I doubt you slept much last night," she offered.

If the Renaissance people were leaving tomorrow, then he'd rather go now. She was right, though—his head pounded and his eyelids were starting to feel like hundred-pound bales of hay sat on them as the adrenaline wore off from his earlier scuffle. "It's probably better not to wait until morning to follow through on this."

Ryan agreed, looking as if he might explode if he didn't get answers soon. His nervous tick of chewing on a tooth-pick had already surfaced.

"I hope you guys find him. This is scary," Samantha

finally said. She reached across the table and squeezed Rebecca's hand.

"He won't surprise us this time," she said. "You be careful, too. Take extra precaution if you're out somewhere alone, day or night."

"I will. Speaking of which, I'd better get back to Dad. He's had a lot on his mind lately with the store. I guess the pressure of owning a business is getting to him more as he ages." She shrugged. "I'm so happy we got to see each other."

"Tell Melanie hello for me."

Brody picked up on a flash in Samantha's eyes. When he really thought about it, Melanie hadn't been back to Mason Ridge since college. "Tell her we'd love to see her sometime."

"Any chance she'll be coming back for the reunion next year?" Rebecca asked.

Samantha flinched, only for a brief moment. If Brody hadn't been watching her, he would've missed it.

"I doubt it," Samantha said. "Melanie doesn't like to come back. She doesn't have great memories from high school and her parents are almost always on the road now. They go see her in Houston."

Brody figured a small town like Mason Ridge wasn't for everybody.

Everyone stood and said their goodbyes. Brody requested the check and covered their lunch and drinks.

"You haven't eaten anything yet," Rebecca said stubbornly when he tried to usher her out the door.

To appease her, he ordered a club sandwich to go. He tried not to think about how nice it was that someone was looking out for him for a change. Experience had taught him being dependent on others could backfire and the burn left a permanent mark.

Brody had always taken care of himself, especially after his mother had pulled her disappearing act. His father had buried himself in work, so Brody learned his way around the kitchen in order to eat. There wasn't much ceremony to it at first, mostly opening cans of soup and making sandwiches. He'd gotten better over time and once he was old enough to man the grill, his dinners got a lot more interesting.

Conversation flowed easily while they waited for his order. Later, he wanted to double check the social media messages and he still hadn't worked through all the threatening letters to see if anything was there. They had a list of suspects, sure, but he needed something to narrow it down. It was too much to hope for a name but that's exactly what he needed. Then, he could fit the rest of the pieces together.

"I'll drive," Ryan said. "We can leave your truck here."

Brody nodded, thanked the waitress and settled the bill. His left hand instinctively reached for the lower part of Rebecca's back as they walked toward the door.

Pulling it back, he held the door open and followed the others to Ryan's SUV.

"My uncle usually leaves his door unlocked when he's home," Ryan offered, trying the handle. It turned, so he opened the door. "He's most likely out back, drinking, if he still lives here."

Brody followed, linking his fingers with Rebecca's. To hell with what Ryan thought. Why did Brody feel guilty about holding her hand? Wasn't like he was making a move on her. And yet, having that link kept his heart from racing. It still pounded for a different reason. The vendors hadn't matched any of the names from the suspect list Brody had checked on the drive to Garland. That trail had gone cold.

He didn't have a list of all vendor employees, so festival workers couldn't be ruled out altogether.

Rebecca took two steps inside and froze. Brody immediately knew why. It was the smell of apple tobacco.

He squeezed her hand, urging her forward. Her hesitation disappeared as she powered ahead.

Inside was dark and sparsely furnished. Blinds were closed, only allowing a smidge of light to push through. An old couch with a couple of mismatched chairs pretty much covered the decor in the living room. There was an old TV with a protruding back sitting on an industrial wooden wire spool. The kitchen was on par with the rest of the place. Greg's house was what most people would call a dedicated bachelor pad. It would work for someone in college, but for a man Greg's age most people would consider the place sad.

"This has to be my uncle's place," Ryan said. "I remember this furniture."

Brody looked for any sign there could've been a child there. Of course, Shane had been gone for fifteen years, so whatever Brody saw wouldn't belong to him. If Greg abducted kids, there should be some evidence.

Nothing stood out.

The door to the back porch creaked as Ryan pushed it open.

"It's me, Uncle Greg." Ryan quickly added, "I brought company."

Uncle Greg was a tall and slight man, and it wasn't lost on Brody that he fit the description of the Mason Ridge

Abductor. His easy smile faded when his gaze stopped on Rebecca.

"What brings you and your friends all the way out here?" he asked, shifting his weight from one foot to the other, looking uneasy. He held tightly to a beer can as he took a swig. "You folks want something to drink?"

"Nothing for us, thanks," Brody said, noticing the tension around Ryan's eyes as he came up beside him. Play this wrong and his uncle might not talk at all.

Rebecca had eased behind Brody a little more, clearly uncomfortable being around Ryan's relative. Her discomfort wasn't full-on panic and Brody took that as a good sign to keep going. If her fingers stiffened any more, he'd excuse them both. There was no reason to put her through anything she didn't want to be part of and he'd wait with her in the SUV. Since she was doing okay, and he really wanted to stick around to see Uncle Greg's reactions to Ryan's questions, Brody stayed.

Ryan continued, "I need to ask you a few questions."

"Take a seat while I refresh my drink," Greg motioned to a mixed grouping of mismatched plastic chairs.

To be polite, Brody did.

"You remember my friends, Brody and Rebecca?" Ryan asked.

"Nice family, the Hughes." Greg popped open a fresh beer from the cooler, took a gulp and sat down next to Ryan.

Brody noted it was the farthest seat from Rebecca. He also noticed that Greg didn't mention anything about his own family. And that was probably for the best.

Rebecca had a death grip on Brody's fingers. He glanced at her to get a read on whether or not he needed to take her to the SUV. Her gaze was intent on Greg. The creased lines on her forehead indicated she was carefully studying him.

The pulse at the base of her throat beat rapidly but that was her only tell. Otherwise, she looked surprisingly calm. Then again, she had the most to gain from this interview.

No reason to leave yet.

"Tell me everything you remember about the night her brother was taken," Ryan pressed.

"I've already told the law everything I knew." Greg's expression dropped to frustration and despair. "Did they believe me? No. They hassled me for months after that boy went missing. I couldn't walk to the corner without being hauled in for loitering."

His expression was genuine. He had the worn look of an innocent man who'd suffered horrendous abuse at the hands of law enforcement. Brody could see Sheriff Brine pulling something like this.

Greg turned directly to Rebecca. He said, "I'm sorry for your loss, ma'am, but I want you to know that I had nothing to do with what happened. I've told the sheriff the same thing. But he didn't listen." He took another gulp of beer and Brody noticed Greg's hands shook. "I don't want to talk about it no more, either. Isn't it enough I moved out of town to get away from all the harassment?"

Brody hadn't thought about the fact that Greg might've been targeted all those years ago. Everyone knew Sheriff Brine disliked the Hunts. Guess he'd taken full advantage of what happened to demonstrate his power.

Ryan comforted his uncle, who was clearly shaken up just remembering.

"I'm the one who's sorry," Rebecca said, rising from her seat. She walked over and hugged Greg. "The sheriff shouldn't have taken advantage of what happened to my family to hurt you."

Greg blinked up at her, clearly stunned by her kindness. "I've done a lot of wrong things in my life but I would never hurt no child. I cried like everybody when that boy went missing."

She patted his shoulder. "I know."

He crossed his legs, the look of surprise still on his aging features. "If you ask me, the sheriff knew more than he let on back then."

Angry words from a man who'd been scorned. Brody couldn't blame the guy for lashing out. It was no secret that Brine didn't like any of the Hunts.

Rebecca thanked him for his time and turned to Ryan and Brody. "We should head back and leave this poor man alone. He's been through enough already."

Brody rose to his feet ahead of Ryan.

They said their goodbyes and moved toward the house.

Brody stopped and picked up the pipe on the plate being used as an ashtray. He turned. "Can I ask you something?"

"Shoot," Greg said, still visibly shaken at the memories of what Sheriff Brine had put him through.

"Why apple tobacco?"

"That's easy. Picked up the habit from an old drinking buddy who used to come to town with the festival." The man didn't flinch.

Greg took another drink and Brody tried his best not to look too interested in the answer to his next question. "Do you remember that guy's name?"

"Sure do. Thomas…oh, what's his name. Something. It's right there on the tip of my tongue." He banged his knuckles on his forehead. "I remember now. Last name was Kramer."

"Thank you. You've been a big help today. We appreciate you being honest with us."

"I do what I can."

"You don't happen to know where Thomas is now, do you?"

"Nah. I don't get to the festival anymore. I try to stay clear of that town with Brine breathing down my neck every time I walk on the sidewalk."

One look at Rebecca said she'd caught on.

They had a name.

"Any chance you can still describe him?" Brody asked.

"Sure," Greg said. "He was my about my height and build. Had brown eyes."

Find Thomas Kramer and they had a shot at finding out what had happened to Shane.

Brody thanked Greg for his time.

By the time the trio reached the SUV, Rebecca looked about to burst. She held it in long enough to open the door and slip inside.

"We have a name," she said.

"We sure do. And he matches the description, too."

"Thomas Kramer. Wasn't he one of the suspects?" Rebecca asked.

Ryan started the SUV, put the ignition into Drive and pulled away from his uncle's house. His worst fears put to rest, he looked relieved for the first time since this ordeal had begun.

"It's familiar." Brody checked his phone. "Sure is."

They owed the encampment a visit. He checked his watch. The festival wouldn't start for hours. It would be more difficult to find Lester with those costumes on.

Brody wished he'd asked what job Thomas Kramer had at the festival.

With this being the last night, Brody had very little time to work with. He wasn't sure it was safe for him to go on his own to the RV park where festival workers kept a close watch.

Based on the protection details they had going, it wouldn't surprise Brody if they carried guns for night duty.

Did they know they'd had a kidnapper among them? Were their efforts to keep out locals like they'd said, or were they protecting their own from a threat within? Lester had said that they'd started patrolling based on the grocery store attack.

In hindsight, their efforts seemed larger than the crime. A local woman was mugged at the grocery store and suddenly they're setting up patrols, attacking anything that moves in the woods?

Seemed like on over-the-top reaction to what the sheriff's office had said was a random occurrence.

Chapter Twelve

This was the closest Rebecca had been to a breakthrough in the case in years—she could feel it. Energy hummed through her at the thought they could be getting close to solving a fifteen-year-old puzzle and possibly finding her brother.

Thoughts buzzed around in her head. If Kramer had been a suspect, why would they have let him go? Wouldn't the sheriff have interviewed him? What about the FBI?

Of course, there were more leads than people to handle them back then. Even at twelve, Rebecca had known that much.

Ryan had been quiet for the entire half-hour trip so far. "My uncle is a drunk. It's possible he's remembering the name wrong."

"I thought about that," Brody said, flashing a knowing look toward Rebecca. "Never hurts to take it seriously, though."

Rebecca knew both men were trying to soften the blow if this turned out to be a nonlead, and she loved them for it.

BY THE TIME Ryan had dropped them at the restaurant where Brody's truck was still parked, Rebecca's thoughts ping-ponged from Thomas Kramer to Brody.

They had a name, Thomas Kramer, and the very real possibility he would lead her to the truth.

For the rest of the ride to Brody's place, she vacillated between excitement and fear. Questions assaulted her. What if they'd found him? What if they hadn't?

What if they wrapped this case and she and Brody walked away from each other for good?

The truth was that she liked being close, having him depend on her. Making sure he ate and didn't overexert himself were things that made her ridiculously happy.

There was something so right about taking care of Brody.

He'd barely set his keys on the table in the foyer when she said, "I'll grab the letters to see if one of them is signed by Kramer."

"While you do that, I'll see if I can find any news about him or an address," Brody said, moving to the laptop in the kitchen.

When he came back into the open-concept room, he brought the laptop with him and moved to the sofa. "It's more comfortable over here if you'd like to join me."

She did, tucking her foot under her bottom as she sat down. They had a name. And she had a feeling this all would be over soon. "We're getting close."

"We don't know if Thomas Kramer is our guy yet. If not, this isn't the end."

Tears rolled down her cheeks despite her best efforts to hold them back. She hadn't expected to get so emotional with him, dammit.

"You told me something the other day and it made a hell of a lot of sense," he said.

Wiping a few tears away, she said, "What was that?"

"Holding in emotion is dangerous. Not talking about

the things that bother us, bottling them up, doesn't lead to anything good. And I think you're putting on a brave front right now."

His words hit home and the floodgates opened. Tears streamed and she couldn't hold them back if she'd tried.

"Get over here," he said.

Rebecca was in his arms before she could recount all the reasons this would be a bad idea, her face buried in his strong chest.

"You're scared and there's nothing wrong with that," he said, his voice a deep, steady timbre. His quiet strength was like the river that cut through granite.

This was the closest she'd been to figuring out the past. Rebecca pulled herself together. "I'll be okay."

She picked up the stack of letters and set them on her lap.

Brody kissed her forehead before opening the file on his laptop.

It didn't take long for him to say, "Look here."

Her heart skipped a beat as she read the screen. "Are those notes from his interview?"

"Looks like it," Brody said. "Did you notice this?"

"He had a child who died at age seven," she said, horrified. "Wouldn't that make him a prime suspect?"

"I would think so," Brody said quickly, his eyes skimming the file. "Here. It says that his alibi checked out and that's why he was cleared of suspicion."

"It says he was caring for a sick aunt that weekend," Rebecca said. "She could've lied for him."

"I'd put money on it."

"Any chance we can find his address?" she asked.

Brody minimized the window on his screen and then

pulled up a search engine. He tapped the keys on the keyboard. "Nothing. Although, his address might not be listed."

"Or he could live with someone else. Another relative," she said.

"True." Brody rocked his head.

"Any chance his aunt's name and address is in that report?" Rebecca's pulse raced in her chest.

Brody pulled up the file and scrolled through the entire page. "It's not here. When we go to the festival tonight, I'll ask Lester about Kramer."

"I feel like we should be doing something more right now," she said, feeling antsy. Answers were close. She could feel it.

"We are," he said. "And we will. I know patience is difficult right now, believe me, but the truth will come out soon enough."

"I want to talk to this Kramer guy."

"We will," he reassured. "Right now, there's not much more we can do until we talk to Lester tonight."

"You're probably right." Her heart trilled against her rib cage and she needed to slow down her breathing, find a way to calm herself.

Looking around Brody's place, at the comfortable decor, she could see herself living in something like this with him. In fact, this was exactly the kind of place she'd live in if she had a ranch. She loved the open space of the landscape, and the Texas sky was nowhere brighter in the day or more majestic at night than in Mason Ridge. Chicago had been wonderful, too, for different reasons. And mostly, it had been different.

Walking down the street there she could be anyone. She was no longer "that girl." No one whispered.

And yet, Mason Ridge would always be home in her heart.

Was it because Brody was there?

"I didn't leave you all those years ago, Brody, so much as run away from here, from everything I felt. I needed to sort out my emotions, but I hurt you in the process. I'm so sorry."

Brody lifted her chin until her face was raised and she looked into his clear blue eyes. She'd expected to find pity in them, but instead she saw something hungry, something primal. Need?

"What time should we leave?" she asked.

"We have a little while. The festival workers will be setting up for opening soon so I doubt we'd get in without a warrant, which we don't have."

"We have a little time to kill?" Rebecca ran her finger along Brody's strong jawline. Neither looked away.

Chapter Thirteen

Brody felt Rebecca's heartbeat pounding against his chest. The rapid rhythm matched his own. With her in his arms, he felt an emotion that was foreign to him—intimacy. And an overwhelming need to pick her up, take her to his bed and show her just how much a woman she'd become overtook him.

He'd experienced need but nothing matching the intensity of this feeling.

Somewhere in the back of his mind, he realized being this close was a bad idea. Staring into her honey-brown eyes, the smell of her shampoo drowning his sense, and all reasoning flew out the window.

Just when he thought he might be able to stop this from going any further, she shifted position enough to pull her shirt over her head and drop it on the floor.

"You can tell me no if you think this is a bad idea, Brody." The way his name rolled off her tongue made him want to hear her say it again and again as his tongue moved down her neck.

She stood and shimmied out of her jeans. Underneath, she wore matching lace panties.

Blood pulsed toward his already uncomfortably stiff length.

He tugged her toward him until she was standing in front of him, his hands to either side of her hips. Leaning forward, he rested his forehead on her stomach. "You have no idea how badly I want to do this."

He looked up at her as she stood there with defiance in her stare.

"But?"

"No buts. I want to make love to you, Rebecca. Now it's your turn to take an out, because I've already made up my mind. If you have any doubts about what we're about to do, you're going to have to be the one to stop this. In about two seconds, I won't be able to so I need to know that you want this. Me."

"It's always been you, Brody. I've always wanted you."

That was all the encouragement he needed. Standing, rising to his full height, he dipped his head down and claimed her mouth. Their lips molded together as he slid his tongue inside her mouth, the need to taste her overtaking every rational thought.

Her hands traveled across his chest, moving upward until they tunneled in his hair, pulling and tugging as her tongue swirled inside his mouth. She tasted so sweet.

His shirt joined hers on the floor.

By the time he reached for the zipper of his jeans, her hands were already there, so he let her do the honors. A second later, his pants were tossed on top of hers.

There in his living room wearing nothing but a bra and panties was the most beautiful woman he'd ever seen. She needed to hear it. "Rebecca, you're gorgeous, sexy."

Thoughts of the innocent kisses they'd stolen in high school were a world away. High school was a world away. And Brody couldn't say he was especially sorry they weren't those same two people they'd been.

He'd grown up, become a man.

His Rebecca, still sweet, had an incredibly sexy side. He'd noticed the way men looked at her. He didn't like it.

"I missed you, sweetheart."

"I'm right here, Brody," she said.

Standing now, he felt an all-too-familiar tug at his heart. Rebecca was the only one who affected him in that way, who reached beyond the mask of strength he wore. With her, he felt a strangely comfortable sense of vulnerability.

This time, he kissed her.

Their mouths moving together, the heat between them rose as his hands moved along her stomach, her breast. He palmed one and her nipple beaded against his palm.

It was her silky bra that hit the floor next. She was all curves and soft skin, and his groin tightened when he really saw her.

Brody took her by the hand and led her to his room.

By the time she was on the bed, all of their clothes littered the floor. *Rebecca on his bed.* He liked the sound of those words more than he should.

"Do you have protection? There hasn't been a need for me to be on the pill," she said.

"That can wait."

On his knees, he ran his finger along the tender flesh of the insides of her thighs. Her body quivered along the stroke of his hands.

"Brody, I want you *now*."

"I have no plans to rush this." It had been a long time since Brody had been interested enough in a woman to take her to bed. He'd stopped doing casual sex.

Looking at Rebecca, at the perfection that was her, everything in his body begged for quick release, but self-discipline was his middle name and he had every intention of enjoying this to the fullest.

"Brody, are you planning to torture me by making me wait?" She sat up, took his arm and tried to urge him toward her. Her face was flush with need, and he felt her body humming with anticipation. "Because I can't."

He smiled at her, moving just out of her reach. She was everything he wanted in a woman—beautiful, intelligent, sexy. And not one female had lived up to the standard she'd set so many years ago.

"As a matter of fact, I had something different in mind." He leaned forward and kissed her to disarm her.

Tucking his hands underneath her sweet round bottom, he tilted her until her head rested on his pillow again.

"No fair…" She pouted until she seemed to realize what he was doing.

She was already wet for him when he inserted three fingers inside her and so he was the one who groaned.

He worked her mound with his thumb as he dipped his fingers again and again, loving the way her body moved and the sensual moans she made.

Pulsing faster, deeper, harder, her muscles clenched and released around his fingers.

"Brody," she whispered breathlessly.

He would never get tired of hearing her say his name.

REBECCA SHOULD BE embarrassed at how quickly she'd climaxed. She wasn't. Everything with Brody seemed right and the sexual tension between them had been building since they'd met up at the coffee shop the other morning. If she were being totally honest, it had been building long before that. In high school, they were too young to really know what it was or do anything about it.

Even though he'd tipped her over the edge once already, she wanted more. She needed to feel his weight on top of her, pressing her into the mattress. Him moving inside her.

She pushed up on her elbows, watching as his shaky hands managed the condom. "You need help with that?"

"I think I got it." He rolled it over his tip.

She reached over and guided it down his large shaft.

His guttural groan at her touch nearly drove her crazy. She wanted him to feel everything he'd just given her and so much more.

Pulling him over her, opening her legs to welcome him, he released a sexy grunt as he drove inside her. She opened her legs more, adjusting to his length.

Her hands mapped the lines of his back, memorizing everything that was Brody, and he thrust deeper, reaching her core. She matched his intensity, craving, needing more and more as they rocketed toward the edge.

He pulled out a little, his tip still inside, and tensed.

"What is it, Brody? What's wrong?"

"Nothing. It feels a little too right and I'm already there. I want this to last."

"Don't stop now. We can always do it again."

His smile faded as he reached the depth of his first thrust. She bucked her hips, needing to fly over the edge with him.

Harder. Faster. Deeper.

More.

Their bodies, twined, exploded with pleasure. A thousand bombs detonated at once, sending volts of electricity and pleasure rocketing through her. She could feel him pulsing inside her as her muscles clenched around his length.

When he'd drained her of the last spasm, he pulled

out and folded on his side next to her. The weight of his
arm over her, his touch, quieted any protest trying to tell
her that this might have been a bad idea. His heart raced,
matching her tempo, as he leaned over and pressed a kiss
to her temple. And then another to her forehead as he
pulled her in closer. His body was soft skin over power-
ful muscle, silk over steel.

She wanted to say the three words roaring through
her mind but stopped herself, refusing to think about the
fact that he had built a life in Mason Ridge and she was
a temporary resident.

Being with Brody was dangerous but far from wrong,
even if it wouldn't last.

BRODY WOKE WITH a start. He'd only dozed off for half
an hour and yet it had felt like so much longer. No doubt
the result of a satisfied sleep that came with the best sex
of his life. Rebecca lay still in his arms, the scent of her
citrus and flowery shampoo filling the air around him.
He could get used to breathing her in, lying next to her
all night. Part of him wished they could stay right there.

The window of opportunity to track down Lester and,
therefore, find Thomas Kramer, was closing.

In a few hours, it would be dark outside and the fire-
works show would begin over the lake, signaling the end
of the weeklong festivities.

The workers would scatter as the break-down crew
went to work. By morning, there'd be nothing left of the
festival but memories. He slowly peeled her arm off him,
careful not to disturb her.

There was enough time for him to make a cup of coffee
and he wanted to let her sleep as long as possible.

It took all the self-discipline he possessed to disengage

himself from her soft, warm body. Drawing on what was left of his willpower, he slipped out of the covers, located his boxers and put them on.

One last look at her while she lay there, her shimmering chestnut hair splayed across the pillow, and everything in his crazy world seemed right.

How long would it last?

Rebecca had been clear. She would leave town and not look back the minute she could.

He turned and walked out of the room.

The coffee was ready in a couple of minutes. His housekeeper had given good advice about stocking the shelves. And he was all right living by himself, wasn't he?

Didn't Brody prefer to do things his way, like keeping his shoes inside the door and not cleaning up the mud right away when it rained? He knew how to take care of himself, how to cook. Weren't those things important to him? He didn't have to explain where he was on a Friday night or defend having an extra beer while he watched the game.

After serving in the military, he'd wanted nothing more than to come home and be part of the community again. He figured he needed to get his bearings first before he tried to build onto his life.

Someday he planned to find the right woman and make their relationship permanent. Kids didn't seem like the worst idea at some point. He didn't care if he had boys or girls so long as they were healthy. Of course, if he had a daughter, he'd want her to look just like Rebecca.

Brody sighed sharply, ignoring the pain in his chest, and booted up his laptop, sipping his fresh brew.

Assessing how far he'd come should make him feel a sense of gratification. The house was comfortable and nice. He had land. His work rehabilitating horses was important and made a difference. He had enough money to be happy but not so much it was all he cared about.

So, why did he suddenly feel there was a gaping hole in his life?

A still-sleepy Rebecca shuffled into the room. "I can't believe I conked out."

"Come sit down. I'll make you a cup of coffee." He'd had time to reach out to a friend in the military about Randy the other morning and had been hoping to hear back. There was no response, which wasn't surprising. It had only been a day. *Give it time, Fields.*

He'd enlisted Dylan's help, as well. Brody would ask for an update when he saw his friend later. Patience racked right up there with second chances. Brody didn't care for either.

"Do we have time?" she asked, stretching. She looked sexy as hell standing in his living room.

"It'll only take a sec." He moved to the kitchen, popped a pod into the coffeemaker and returned a minute later with a fresh cup. "Here you go."

She thanked him with a kiss and a smile. "How's your head?"

"Better." He motioned for her to join him at the table.

"This coffee is fantastic." She was sitting on the edge of the seat, looking nervous.

Did she regret sleeping with him? He almost laughed out loud. That would be a new one. Wasn't he always the one keeping one foot out the door in every relationship since her? High school crushes hardly counted. Maybe he'd held everyone at a safe distance since his mother had ditched him. Brody hadn't had a horrible childhood. He and his father had been close, two bachelors under the same roof. His father had worked long hours to dig them out of the hole created by his mother.

Brody shoved those thoughts aside as he rose. "I'm going to hop in the shower before we leave. Care to join me?"

The smirk on Rebecca's lips was sexy as hell as she took his hand. "I'd love to, Mr. Fields."

After making love again, Brody dressed, thinking twice wasn't nearly enough. Could this, whatever *this* was, morph into something more permanent? He couldn't go there yet. What he could manage was enjoying what they had for today.

And he didn't have a whole lot of time to consider much of anything else considering time ticked away on finding Thomas Kramer. Brody's internet search had turned up unlucky. Then again, he hadn't expected to find Kramer easily. This guy had avoided capture for fifteen years. He traveled with a festival that was on the road forty-five weeks out of the year and could live anywhere.

Dawson texted that he was already at the festival with Ryan looking for Lester, and that Dylan was coming with Maribel. Said that Dylan had some news for Rebecca that he wanted to deliver in person. Brody hoped he knew what that meant. He wanted to keep a smile on her beautiful face.

"Think we have time to swing by and see my mother on our way? I spoke to her nurse earlier and Mother's having a good day. She had a great visit with Chelsea and Kevin this morning and they promised to stay in touch. They left their information with Mother. I guess having company did wonders for her," Rebecca said, entering the room. She'd dressed in a light blue tank top, jeans and sandals.

"It's on the way to the festival grounds, so that's not a problem." He withheld the information about Dylan's news. No sense getting excited about it before they knew what it was. Dawson had been tight-lipped so far.

"I'm ready if you are."

He nodded as her ringtone sounded in her purse. She retrieved her phone and checked the screen. "It's my dad. Do you mind if I take this?"

"Not at all." Brody smiled. From all he'd known, Mr. Hughes was a good guy. He deserved to know his daughter.

"Hi, Dad," she said into the phone, moving to sit on the couch in the next room. "I'm good. Thank you for calling." A beat of silence passed. "I'd love to come see you and the boys." Another hesitation. "Next Sunday? Barbecue?" She glanced toward Brody.

"Good idea," he whispered, just loud enough for her to hear.

"Would you mind if I brought someone?" Her eyes flashed toward Brody again. "Good. See you at six. Sure, I'll bring a swimsuit."

There was a moment of silence followed by, "I know I haven't said this in far too long. I love you, Dad."

She closed the phone and turned to Brody. "What are you doing next weekend?"

"Taking you to a barbecue." If she needed him there to ease her way back into her father's life, Brody didn't mind helping out. It was the right thing to do and he felt good about encouraging the reunion. Not everyone had a relationship with a parent worth holding on to. If someone did, they needed to grab hold with both hands and hang on for the ride. Those first steps toward the starting gate were often the hardest to take. "For what it's worth, I'm proud of you."

"You probably don't want to hear this from me, Brody." She glanced down to the floor and then back up at him. "I think you're a great man."

His heart skipped a beat because he thought she was going to say something else, the three words he wasn't ready to hear. Because when this was over, he had every intention of walking away.

REBECCA WAS HAPPY she didn't have to coax Brody to go inside with her to see her mother. Panic had engulfed Rebecca when they'd gone to her room only to find it empty. Turned out, her mother was in the recreation room playing a game of chess with another patient, looking pleased she'd made a friend.

They'd cut their visit short, promising to return the following day. Her mother had made Brody vow he'd return soon, too. Then she'd thanked him for looking after her daughter so well.

Since the festival was a short drive, Rebecca didn't argue when Brody made a move to drive again.

Neither said much on the ride over. Tensions rose the closer they got. Brody parked near Main Street and then texted the others to let them know he and Rebecca were there. It didn't take long to find Ryan and Dawson.

"We found our friend, Lester, from earlier," Dawson said. "He said Thomas Kramer was part of the breakdown crew. Or at least he had been until last year when they'd found him peeking through windows of the workers' RVs."

Rebecca couldn't help but think Kramer would have to be strong to do that job.

A text came from Dylan saying he was delayed with Maribel and would join them as soon as he could.

"Another reason their guard has been so high?" Brody asked.

"Exactly. Lester was up-front with us, but we both got the impression he was uncomfortable talking about one of his own," Ryan added.

"If they fired him last year, why come back? Why follow them here?" Brody asked, taking Rebecca's hand.

She wondered if the sudden urge to keep her close by came with knowing Kramer could be right next to them and they wouldn't know it. "Good question," Ryan said.

Dawson nodded. "I told Dylan I'd stick around the midway area. I'll keep watch. You guys should check the perimeter and see if he's hanging around, watching for another target."

Brody agreed.

Rebecca looked around, remembering the timing of Chelsea and Kevin's son's disappearance. "I wonder if they suspected him of the Sunnyvale kidnapping and that's why they beefed up their own security. It had happened on the last day of the festival last year."

Brody nodded. "There have been reports of him showing up in other places, but our guy says he hasn't seen Kramer," Dawson said.

"I ran a search of abductions of seven-year-old boys in the area and there haven't been many in the past fifteen years," Brody said.

"Maybe those are the only ones here." Rebecca didn't want to think about the truth in front of her. If Kramer had been the one to take Shane and he was still hurting boys, then it stood to reason that Shane was dead.

Chapter Fourteen

"I keep wondering why he'd come back. He had to know he'd be figured out eventually," Rebecca said as she, Ryan and Brody walked the perimeter of the festival while Dawson waited on the midway.

Brody didn't like the answers he came up with. "It's been a long time in between abductions here. Plus, he's bold because he's done a great job of hiding his activities so far. He knows this area, the woods. He's been able to slip under the radar all these years. But his time is up. We know who he is. He's going down and it's only a matter of time before we find him."

She paused, releasing a heavy breath. "Do you think it's possible that Shane's still…"

"I do. And you have to believe it, too." He didn't want to tell her what he thought Dylan's news would be just in case he was wrong. Brody and Ryan exchanged knowing glances.

Brody checked the surroundings. They were stopped near a farm road toward the back of the festival grounds. There were no residential developments for a good two miles on either side of them. He only had one bar on his phone.

Ryan pointed to a fresh trail that had been cut through

the brush. "Someone's been here. Could be teenagers looking for a party spot, or…" His gaze bounced from Rebecca to Brody.

Teens were known for searching out good places to build a bonfire and drink near the county line. And this had all the right markings for it.

"Except this trail has been trimmed and they don't normally use anything sharp," Brody pointed out, examining the marks.

"This might be another wild-goose chase, but it's worth looking into," Ryan said.

"Let's check it out. We can notify the sheriff if it's worth his time. I'm sure his office has been inundated with leads since the sketch hit the air."

Ryan nodded. "True."

Rebecca, on the other hand, remained perfectly still. Her face had gone pale. Brody didn't like having her along, but he didn't figure she'd let him go without her. He linked their fingers and took a step forward.

She followed until they moved into the tree line. She stopped, refusing to budge, except to grip his hand like death.

"Hold on a second, Ryan." Concerned, Brody turned his full attention to her. "What is it, Rebecca?"

She stood frozen for a long moment. "Do you smell that?"

"What?"

Ryan moved to Brody's side.

"I know that smell." Fear widened her eyes; the color drained from her face, and her fingers were icy cold.

"What is it, Rebecca?"

"Apple tobacco." Her moment of hesitation dissolved like salt in boiling water. Her gaze narrowed and her lips thinned as determination replaced fear. She stalked toward the woods.

Brody and Ryan kept close beside her, flanking her, as the sun kissed the treetops. She needed space and Brody intended to give it to her. Enough to work out her anger, but not so much as to leave her exposed.

Rage burned through Brody with each forward step. Even though the light was beginning to fade, he saw a small building positioned in the trees ahead coming into focus.

Rebecca had to have seen it, too. She didn't stop charging ahead. In fact, she increased her pace. Not a good idea. He couldn't let her be the first one to see what was inside that place.

Everything inside Brody wanted to stop her, to protect her from what he feared would come next. They could be walking up on a body, even Jason's from last year.

That there was no stench in the air was the only positive sign this might not go south.

He squeezed Rebecca's hand for support and exchanged a look with Ryan. She seemed to understand the need to move slowly and quietly, just in case Thomas Kramer was inside. Or watching from somewhere in the woods, setting another trap.

Brody would've liked time to gather intel before storming into the building, set a perimeter.

Instead, he signaled for the others to stop and listen.

There was no noise coming from the broken-down old shed..

A chill raced up Brody's back as he surveyed the area. The trees were thick enough to conceal the building, which was large enough to house a few people and supplies. "Hold position while I try to get a visual."

Rebecca and Ryan nodded.

This was exactly the kind of location Thomas Kramer would use. An abandoned shed in the woods that had been long forgotten. Unfortunately, there were far too many places like this in and around Collier County.

The suburban sprawl spreading from Dallas had not reached this place. And that was a large part of the reason Brody had returned. The other incentive had been to stay close to his father.

A little voice said he came back to be close to Rebecca, but he shut that down.

That same irritating voice said he came back because he still had feelings for her.

Was there any possibility that was true?

No.

Did he feel something when Rebecca was around? Yes.

Love?

Brody shoved the word down deep as he moved stealthily through the woods. *Loyalty* was better.

The shed door had a place for an outside lock, which meant the original owner most likely had kept small farming equipment inside at some point. Brody inched closer without so much as snapping a twig. He didn't want to give away his location should Kramer be inside. Surprise was the best advantage and Brody had a lump on the back of his head to prove it.

There was no lock. Either the place was clean or they were about to walk into a trap.

Brody's need to protect Rebecca overrode his rational mind, because his first thought was to breach the building alone. No way did he want her within five feet of that shed. He circled back to her and Ryan.

"You sure you want to do this?" he asked.

She nodded. "Did you find anything?"

"There's no lock on the door. We shouldn't have any trouble getting inside." He hesitated. "I do want to remind you this could be a setup. Or you might end up seeing something you can't erase from your mind. I'd prefer to go first."

"I thought about that," she said ominously.

"And you still want to go in with me?" He looked her straight in the eyes. Any fear, any hesitation, and he'd go on his own. "Ryan can stay here with you."

Her head was already shaking, and Brody noticed that her body was, too.

"I can't live my life afraid anymore," she said.

As much as he wanted to stop her, to talk some reasoning into her for staying back, he couldn't. He understood her need to face her fears. Hell, he'd done the same thing. When his Humvee had been hit by an RPG, he'd volunteered for the next mission just so he'd have a chance to climb back in one and drive down that same street. He knew if he didn't, he might as well go home. In his eyes, being useless to the men who depended on him would be far worse than dying.

Brody linked his fingers with Rebecca's and led her toward what could be her worst nightmare. If she was ready to face her past, could they think about starting things up again? The thought caught him off guard. Did he want another chance with Rebecca?

Up to now, he'd convinced himself that he'd accepted this assignment for unselfish reasons, for her. Had he done it for himself all along?

Not ready to process that information, he tucked it away and moved to the door. He'd give her one last chance to reconsider. "Ready?"

BRODY AND RYAN moved like a well-rehearsed team, Ryan against Brody's back, insuring no one could surprise them from any angle. The two barely needed words between them to know what to do, their connection was so strong.

It wasn't so long ago that she and Brody had shared the same unspoken communication link. Had the years changed him or was he holding back with her because she'd hurt him? She'd felt the sparks between them, they'd made love, and she wondered if that could grow into anything more.

And yet, she knew that wasn't possible.

Good relationships were based on trust and communication. Without trust, good communication was impossible.

And above all, Brody valued loyalty.

She stood in front of the shed, her body trembling, and she wondered if it had anything to do with Brody as much as her fear. Yes, she was scared of seeing what was on the other side of that door. But the determined part of her kicked in and all she could see were Chelsea and Kevin's faces, their pain. The same expression had haunted her mother for so long.

Rebecca knew firsthand how devastating not knowing could be. Shane's disappearance, the years spent searching for him, had branded her. The situation had become worse when her father decided it was time to give up and move on. He'd said he didn't want to live in the past any longer. The same hadn't been true for her mother. She'd sworn she wouldn't rest until she found her son alive or brought his body home. On some level, she must've seen her husband's willingness to put the past behind them as a betrayal to their son, to her. Whatever love had existed between them had fractured. Her mother's relentless dedication to putting up new signs year after year had worn her father down even after their split. He'd said her activity was a slap in the face. He'd cry and say he was sorry that he couldn't bring their son back.

Rebecca didn't blame her father. She figured he was surviving the best he could under the circumstances.

Kevin and Chelsea's love for each other seemed to run deeper. Instead of standing on opposite sides of the room, they stood together. He'd been ready to catch her when she'd fallen. No matter the outcome of their case, Rebecca believed that couple would survive.

They were strong.

It was a safety net she'd never known as a child. Up to now Rebecca had believed relationships couldn't stand the test of time, not when something really bad happened, because of what had materialized with her own parents. And that made it harder to trust in her relationships.

Maybe there was hope for real love, a true connection.

Brody slowly opened the door. What was left of daylight filled the empty space.

That there was no stench had been a comfort. She knew they weren't going to find bodies.

Was anyone inside? It was too quiet. Another piece of her heart broke off that this would be another dead end.

Brody and Ryan stood in front of her, blocking her view. No doubt they felt the need to shield her from whatever horror might be inside the building.

"What's in there?" Rebecca asked as she tried to brace herself for whatever waited on the other side of that door.

"I'll keep watch out here in case he decides to come back to check on this spot," Ryan said, turning to place his back against the wall.

"Someone's been here." Brody took a deep breath and stepped aside.

There was just enough daylight left to see clearly. Bugs flew around her. She slapped her left bicep and then her leg. Mosquitos seemed to be everywhere, poised to take advantage of a quick meal. Dusk was a feeding frenzy.

Flies buzzed around her ears. Rebecca scarcely noticed. Her gaze was intent on the space she'd just stepped into. There was rope on the floor and empty juice boxes in the corner. Her legs almost gave when she took a step closer as horrible memories assaulted her.

"Yes, he has," she said through chattering teeth.

Brody palmed his cell and checked his screen. "According to my map, Mason Ridge Lake isn't far from here. He most likely wouldn't walk there and back, so there might be a source closer. Hold on, let me zoom in. Okay, we have a farmhouse about forty yards from here. Maybe they saw something."

"He was freaked out by me being there. Kept mumbling that I wasn't supposed to be around." Shivers rocked her body just thinking about it. She'd worked to erase those memories for so long.

Before she could ask, Brody was beside her. His arm around her waist steadied her.

"Ryan, call it in. There might be DNA evidence that can positively identify him," Brody called out. He turned to her and said, "Step lightly out of here. The sheriff won't be happy we've trampled all over their evidence."

"They've never been able to find his DNA before," she said. "He's clever."

"These aren't fresh. But, he might not have had time to wipe the place clean." Brody pointed to the empty juice cartons. "And they should be able to identify the child based on those."

Good point. Identifying a child and possibly Kramer would go a long way toward making sure this never happened again.

Brody helped her outside and held on to her while they waited for the sheriff to arrive. "That bothers me."

"What?" Rebecca asked.

"That they weren't able to find DNA evidence before."

"He's too smart," Rebecca said.

"Which doesn't exactly jibe with the theory of a transient. Kramer's tricky. I wonder what else he's has done."

"None of it has to make sense to us. We're normal people and this guy is a calculating monster," Rebecca said. "But the other issue I have is whether or not the sheriff will believe us. He could brush us off and say this could be from anyone."

"Unless the DNA on the juice boxes matches a missing kid in the database," Brody said.

Rebecca nodded, thinking about Jason and his parents, the agony of waiting.

Ryan's gaze moved from Brody's arm to his face. "You sure that you two waiting around here is a good idea?"

"We should head back to the festival. He could be there right now," Brody said.

"Absolutely not. I don't want to leave. Not until we have answers," Rebecca argued.

"Ryan makes a good point. There's nothing we can do to help. In five minutes, the place will be crawling with law enforcement, and we need to give them space to do their jobs."

As much as she wanted to protest, that made sense. Ryan's head was rocking back and forth in agreement, too. Plus, the sheriff didn't exactly believe her most of the time, anyway. Maybe it would be best if she was out of sight. "Okay, but let's walk the woods. Maybe there's another place nearby he stashed someone."

Brody shook his head. "He's gone. He wouldn't stick around."

"But we're so close. He was here. What if he—"

Brody's arm tightened around her waist. He leaned down and said, "I can only imagine what you must be going through. I'm so sorry."

He whispered other reassuring words—words that steadied her racing pulse.

"It's just that we're so close. I can feel it. He was here at some point, which means he comes back."

"He doesn't know we're onto him. And he won't have time to disappear before we find him this time. We're closing in. Plus, others are looking for him. He can't hide with the festival workers anymore. If he's around, we'll find him."

True. She knew that. But everything inside her wanted to keep looking for him in the woods.

She could hear footsteps and radio noise getting louder. "They're coming."

"I didn't think it would take long since they're close by, watching over the festival," Brody said.

Ryan gave Brody a bear hug first and then hugged her. "I'll stick around and give them a statement. You two get back to the festival."

"You sure?" Brody asked.

Seeing the exchange between close friends struck her in a place very deep. She thought about what Brody had said a million times about some families being made from the heart instead of shared tissue. He was right about that.

And a lot of other things, too. Most of all, he was right that no matter how much her heart ached to be close to him again, it was impossible to go back. Even though her pulse still raced with every brush of his arm against her.

And her heart beat heavy in her chest.

Because she also knew she would never feel like this toward another man for as long as she lived.

BY THE TIME she and Brody had finished walking the perimeter of the festival grounds with no luck Ryan had texted to say he was on the midway with the others.

Dylan walked up to the group with his daughter in tow as they arrived.

After hugs and greetings, Rebecca focused on the little girl to take her mind off Jason, Shane and the horrors that lay in the woods. Maribel had Dylan's bold green eyes. She also possessed his dark hair with curls.

Maribel beamed up at Rebecca and her heart literally melted.

Bending down to eye level, Rebecca said, "I've known your daddy since I was this tall." She held her hand up around four feet off the ground.

"Really?" Eyes wide, rosy round cheeks, Maribel was a cherub incarnate. Her *r* came out as a *w* and it was about the cutest thing Rebecca had ever heard.

"It's true. You look a lot like him."

Maribel took a step toward Rebecca and threw her pudgy little arms around Rebecca's neck.

Rebecca hugged the little angel back. She heard Dylan say something about Maribel normally being shy with new people.

Dylan inclined his chin toward the cotton-candy stand. Ryan took the little girl's hand and led her out of earshot.

Wiping away a loose tear, Rebecca said, "She's beautiful, Dylan. You did good."

"I'm lucky," Dylan agreed, but the look in his eyes said he was ready to change the subject. "You want to sit down over there?" He motioned toward a bench.

"No. I'm fine. What is it?" The seriousness in his expression tightened a coil inside her stomach.

A look passed between Dylan and Brody, causing an ominous chill to skitter across her nerves.

"Tell me," she said.

"It looks like I found him."

"Shane?" Surely her ears were playing tricks on her. Dylan couldn't possibly mean her brother.

"We believe it's him." Dylan nodded.

Brody was by her side, his warmth and his touch the only things keeping her upright.

"I have a contact in the military who found the name Brody gave us, Randy Harper. I had an idea which branch he might be in because Dawson took me back to that restaurant outside of town, Mervin's Eats. I brought Maribel, figuring we could gain the hostess's trust easier if my daughter came along. It worked. The hostess started talking about a friend of hers who'd dated him up until the time he left for the service. She couldn't remember his name or which branch, so I asked her to call her friend, and she did."

Air whooshed from Rebecca's lungs as she tried to let his words sink in. Could they have found Shane? Was it even possible after all these years? Tears were already streaming down her cheeks and she didn't bother to wipe them away. They were glorious tears of release. Tears that had been held inside far too long. Tears that needed to be set free. "Where is he?"

"All we know right now is that he's alive. He's in the army out on a mission. I'm told he's a great soldier."

"How can you be sure it's him?"

"We won't know for sure until he takes a DNA test but she said he had a birthmark that looked like Oklahoma on top of his right foot."

"That has to be him. What are the chances someone else would have that?"

"He doesn't remember much of his younger years. She said it bothered him because he'd been told his whole life that his parents had been killed in an accident, that he'd been sent to live with his Uncle Kramer on the road, and that he was an only child but he could swear he had an older sister."

Rebecca dropped to her knees, put her face in her hands and cried.

Everyone gave her space, even Brody. He seemed to know she needed a minute.

The release was sweet as she finally let go. *Shane, my baby brother, you're alive. You remember me. I've missed you so much.*

When she could stem the flow of emotion, she wiped her face and stood. "What else?"

"That's all I know for now. We're waiting for DNA confirmation, but that could take a little while since he's deployed. My contact says we can make contact when he returns to base."

"Do we know when that will be?"

"Sorry. That information is classified. My contact had no idea. My guess is a couple of days to a week at the most."

Rebecca threw her arms around Dylan's neck. "I don't know how to thank you. All of you."

"Us finally helping you has been a long time coming," Dylan said, hugging her back.

Maribel ran up with a big pink cloud-like puff on a stick. "Da-da!"

Rebecca took a step back and laughed as the little girl plowed into her father's legs with her cotton candy. He picked her up, not paying any mind to the pink splotches left on his jeans. Brody was right. Seeing Dylan with his daughter, the tenderness in his eyes, made her believe people could change for the better. She'd always loved her friend, but he was the last person she'd expected to see with a baby on his arm. "Seeing you with your daughter makes me think about life a little differently."

Dylan smiled one of those wide and genuine smiles. "Guess I never knew real love before."

Rebecca had. "You hold on tight to it."

"Yes, ma'am."

The little girl wiggled out of his arms and squealed as she ran through her dad's legs.

Brody and the others formed a protective circle around Maribel. He pulled Rebecca closer as his gaze surveyed the area. He had to know what she was thinking...*he's still out there.*

Chapter Fifteen

"We need to find Lester. Maybe we can pin him down for information about Kramer's whereabouts," Brody said, his frustration outlined in his sharp sigh. "He might know where his aunt lives and I have a feeling Lester didn't tell us everything."

"All I keep wondering is if his aunt lied to authorities before."

Brody's lips thinned. "I want to know why she would do that."

"It's a good deception. Places him away from the scene, gives him an alibi, and he gets free rein. Heck, he could've given her something to knock her out without her even knowing. I wouldn't put anything past a man like that."

Brody stopped suddenly. "That's him. That's Lester right there."

"The guy with the white streak in his hair?"

"Yes. Come on." Brody clasped her hand tighter, as though he knew she needed the extra support. Every step closer to finding Kramer tightened the coil in her stomach. How could the man who'd taken away her brother and ripped her family apart so easily slip through the system?

She wasn't crazy and she was so close to being able to prove it. The man who'd haunted her for fifteen years was real and he was right there in Mason Ridge. "Kramer was ruled out as a suspect too easily back then. We have to find that bastard and bring him to justice." Dare she hope they would find Jason? That Shane seemed to be alive and well was an encouraging sign. Rebecca said a prayer that the little boy was out there, somewhere close by, safe. She tried not to think about the fact that he'd missed a birthday with his family, or how many her brother had. A thought struck her. "I must've gotten too close when I found Shane—Randy online. That's why Kramer came back for me."

"Makes me think he won't leave until he finishes the job," Brody said. "We can't risk it, though. If he figures out we're this close, he could disappear."

Brody touched Lester's shoulder. The guy spun around a little too quickly, his eyes wild.

"Sorry, it's just me," Brody said.

Relief washed over Lester's features, but he tried to play it off. "No problem. We're all a little jumpy with this being the last night. So far, so good, though."

"This is my friend Rebecca," Brody said, introducing her.

After they'd shaken hands, he continued. "Thomas Kramer abducted her and her brother fifteen years ago. She got away, but they never found Shane."

Was Brody intentionally putting names and faces to the story? Lester's expression softened.

"I wish I could help you out, man. No one knows where he is."

"So you're saying that you haven't seen him at all?" Brody pressed.

Lester's gaze moved from Rebecca back to Brody. "Not me personally. One of the guys believes he did."

"Here?"

"Yeah. Earlier, though. I've been watching out ever since," Lester continued. "We put extra eyes on the campsite, too."

"That's smart. Just in case."

"Sorry to hear about your family," Lester said to Rebecca.

"My mom took things really hard. She never recovered." It was true. Rebecca also wanted to play the sympathy card in case this guy was holding back information.

"Kramer's aunt lied for him. Do you have any idea where she lives?" Brody kept pushing.

"I have a kid of my own, a little girl. I can't imagine." Lester paused. "His aunt Sally doesn't live far from here. She's in Brighton. It's why we're extra careful here and in Sunnyvale."

"You must've heard what happened last year," Brody said, glancing at Rebecca.

She made the connection, too. Randy Harper was from Brighton.

Lester nodded.

"Did you know Kramer very well?" Rebecca asked.

"We thought we did. Apparently not."

"According to the police report, he had a son who died," Brody said.

"We didn't know until years later about that. Way after the fact. It all started to make sense then."

"When exactly did you figure this out?" Brody asked.

Lester shrugged. "Not sure exactly. Heard it through the grapevine and couldn't be too sure of the source."

"And you didn't think to go to the police with it?" Rebecca fired back.

"No," he said with a look of apology. "We thought it

was all hearsay. Plus, if we don't run a tight ship then we don't get invited to places. None of us wanted to be associated with a person who abducts children. We couldn't afford to have that hanging over our festival. None of us would have a job."

"Even so, why didn't anyone come forward?" Rebecca asked. "That kind of information is pretty damning, don't you think?"

"We didn't know for sure it was him. Besides, we believed that he was caring for his aunt."

"Didn't you suspect anything when he suddenly showed up with a kid on the road?" Rebecca asked, mustering the kindest voice she could under the circumstances. The coil was tightening and it was becoming unbearable.

"That's the thing, he didn't. Not for a few years, anyway, and we didn't put it together back then. All of a sudden he would talk about his kid going to school, or playing some kind of sport. We figured we just didn't know him well enough to get personal before," Lester said.

"If he didn't take the kid on the road, then where'd he keep him?" Brody asked the question that was on Rebecca's mind.

"Must've been with his aunt Sally," Lester said. "I actually know her address. It's where we used to send his checks."

He pulled up her name on his contacts list from his phone.

Brody entered the information into his cell, and then thanked Lester as he and Rebecca made a run for the truck.

"Now that we have her address, we need to pay her a visit," he said.

"Do you think it's best to investigate without involving the sheriff?" Rebecca asked.

"Even if I trusted his judgment—and I'm not saying I do—the sheriff has to work within the law. We don't. And I have every intention of using whatever means necessary to make her talk. If that's where Kramer took Shane, then it stands to reason he'd take Jason there, too."

"You think we'll find Kramer there?"

"It's possible. If not, we might find a clue as to where he's hiding. All we need is a receipt or motel bill."

She didn't want to think about how relieved she was that the bogeyman who'd haunted her for a decade and a half had a face and a name. No longer was he a larger-than-life figure in a young girl's imagination. He was flesh and blood. Evil, but a man, nonetheless. And men could be taken down.

She glanced up and was startled to realize Brody was watching her as they ran. No doubt, her concern played out on her features.

"I know what you're thinking and we'll get him." Brody's words were spoken with a silent promise as they made it to the truck.

"We find him, we might find out what exactly happened to Shane. I have to think Kramer didn't do anything to hurt my brother, not now that I know he's grown and in the military. Plus, he seems to be taking these boys in an attempt to replace the son he lost."

She paused, trying to let that sink in.

"It makes sense. We don't have the details yet but it wouldn't surprise me to learn that he cared for Shane in the way he wished he could've for his own son."

"I hope DNA confirms that it is Shane for more than selfish reasons. I'd like to give that to my mom. She's been holding on so long. I want her to know what happened to her son, that he's alive." Tears welled in Rebecca's eyes. One broke free and spilled down her cheek. "I need so badly to tell her we found him, but I want to wait until we're one hundred percent sure. Otherwise, we'd break her heart again and she can't take that."

"Shane's alive. Believe it. And we'll get confirmation soon enough."

Brody climbed into the driver's seat and programmed his GPS with the address of Kramer's aunt.

"There isn't a day that goes by that I don't wish he'd kept me and set Shane free." More tears fell as she buckled her seat belt. She needed to tell Brody everything she remembered, to let it go. "We were so scared, but somehow I figured out that my bindings were loose. Shane was upset, crying, so Kramer was in a hurry when he put me back into my shed and he didn't tie me securely. It took me a minute to realize what had happened. He'd taken Shane to another building to calm him. It was dark outside and I remember my legs giving out as soon as I left the shed. I went looking for Shane. I thought if I could get to him, then maybe we could both get away. I was in shock. I couldn't believe I was free." She paused to stop the sobs. "When I couldn't find him, I thought if I could get away and go get help that we'd get back in time."

A few more tears flooded her eyes. She didn't realize she'd been squeezing her hands together until her fingers hurt.

"It's okay. You don't have to talk about this now," Brody soothed, guiding the truck onto the main road.

"I need to do this, Brody. I've been holding it in far too long. It feels good to finally let it out, to really breathe."

"Take it slow. Stop if you need to." He kept his steady gaze on the road in front of them.

"I got lost in the woods. I remember wandering around, afraid to make noise, stop or sleep. By the time they found me, I was dehydrated and delirious. The sheds had been cleared. Everything had been moved. Shane was gone. The monster who took my brother had disappeared." Sobs racked her, so she didn't fight them.

Saying the words made everything real. Being with Brody was different. He made it safe to open up those old wounds. He made her want to let go of the pain and finally talk about it.

She needed to hold on to the feeling while it lasted because as soon as this case was over, he'd be out of her life again. When she could return Shane to her mother, Rebecca would move away from this town and start a new life for herself.

Talking about the past was the first step toward letting it go.

Brody reached out to her with his free hand, patting hers but saying nothing. His touch was more reassuring than any words ever could be. His hand quickly returned to the wheel.

"And you already know we never found out exactly what happened to my brother until now. He was declared dead ten years ago but it felt so hollow. There was no body. No memorial service. Even after the declaration, my mom refused to accept it. She kept vigil. She talked about him like he'd walk through that door any minute and surprise us all. She made a birthday cake for him every year and brought out old photos."

More sobs came.

Brody just sat there, silently reassuring her.

"For years after she'd see him places—on the playground, driving away in the backseat of cars at the gas station, on a school bus. With every anniversary of his disappearance, those news articles would run, and she'd relive what had happened all over again. And yet, she never gave up hope of finding him. Now, he's alive and she deserves to know what happened to her son."

SITTING THERE, listening to Rebecca as she told her story, without being able to take away her pain or make the jerk who'd hurt her pay for his sin, was a knife stab to Brody's chest. Justice was coming, though. Even if this lead didn't pan out, Brody would find a way.

Hearing the words, the raw pain, seeing how Rebecca kept the weight of the world on her shoulders frustrated him to no end. He'd told her before but it was worth repeating. "None of this was ever your fault."

"I know."

"You were just a kid. We were just kids. You did the best you could to survive. That's all any of us can do."

She mumbled something else in agreement and he had to grip the wheel from wanting to reach out and touch her again. He was on a slippery slope with Rebecca, sliding downhill fast. There were no branches to grab on to, nothing to save him. His heart was falling down that sinkhole called love and nothing inside him could gain purchase to stop it on the way down.

They'd driven straight for an hour and a half when the GPS indicated they were getting close to their destination.

Brody slowed the vehicle when he entered the cul-de-sac. He parked two houses down as he watched a tall, thin man exit the ranch-style house.

Kramer?

Rebecca reached for Brody's hand and then squeezed.

The man took the driver's seat of a green sedan.

He was too far away to be able to tell for certain that it was Kramer.

Until the sedan slowed as it neared them and the driver saw Rebecca.

His expression said everything they needed to know. And then he accelerated, his tires squealing as they struggled to gain traction.

"It's him," Rebecca said, her voice no longer shaky with fear. "I saw his face."

Pride filled Brody as he banked a U-turn in the cul-de-sac and sped to Kramer's bumper.

Dark eyes stared at them from the rearview mirror.

"He makes it onto the highway and there's a good chance we'll lose him," Brody said. "Make sure your seat belt is secure."

"Catch him, Brody."

Kramer turned onto a farm road.

Brody maintained a safe distance without allowing Kramer too much leeway.

A few turns and they were following him onto a gravel road.

"He knows this area," Brody said. And Kramer was using it to his advantage as he maintained break-neck speed.

Brody's truck was heavier. He floored the gas pedal, trying to keep up.

Kramer must've panicked because his car veered left and then right. He cut through a corn field and then circled around toward the street they'd been on before.

Any number of innocent people could get hurt if Kramer was allowed to get back on a main road.

Brody gunned the engine, pulling beside Kramer, trying to force him off the road.

In response, Kramer drove his speed up past the hundred-mile-an-hour mark.

The two-lane road was empty, save for Brody and Kramer. That could change any second. Brody had to decide if he should keep pushing the limit, or drop back and follow. But then what? Allow this man to get away? To reach the highway?

Brody gunned the engine, keeping pace with the sedan, and then nudged the wheel right.

Kramer twisted his, jerking the vehicle away from Brody a second before their side panels collided. Then, Kramer overcorrected and his vehicle flew out of control. He sideswiped a tree and was sent into a death spin.

Another tree brought a sudden stop to the deadly rollover. The sound was deafening. The blaze ignited instantaneously.

By then, Brody's truck was at a complete stop.

"Stay here," he said to Rebecca, who was already barreling toward the inferno.

She kept going.

All he could do at that point was try to catch up with her.

The blast that came next caused them both to freeze.

Brody reached for Rebecca's hand. She spun around and buried her face in his chest as they both fell to the ground.

"It's over," she said, tears streaking her cheeks. "It's finally over."

They stayed long enough to give statements to law enforcement and learn that an officer had been sent to the aunt's house. No one was said to be home.

Once in the truck, Rebecca put her hand on Brody's arm as he cranked the engine.

"Can we go there?" she asked. "I need to see for myself that Jason isn't there."

Brody nodded.

Twenty minutes later, he pulled into the familiar cul-de-sac.

Rebecca made it to the door first and knocked. Lights were out and everything was completely quiet. It didn't appear that anyone was home, just as the officer had reported.

"We can ask the neighbors who lives here. Maybe one of them will know something," Brody offered.

"That's a good idea actually. Surely, someone has seen something," she said, spinning around and heading toward the opposite house.

A middle-aged woman answered on the second round of knocking. Rebecca introduced herself and Brody. He hung back a little so as not to intimidate the woman.

"We're sorry to bother you, but we're trying to reach our friend Thomas Kramer. Is this still his address?" Rebecca pointed to the house in question.

The woman gave an odd look. "Do you mean Thomas Harper?"

Harper? Brody made the connection to Randy's last name.

Rebecca must have, too, based on the way her shoulders stiffened.

"Right, sorry. Having one of those days," Rebecca hedged, recovering her earlier demeanor.

"I'm Patricia and yes, that's his house," she confirmed. "Doesn't look like anyone's home. He travels most of the time for work. His little boy comes to visit sometimes."

"And his aunt?" Rebecca asked.

"Never saw a woman around." She shrugged. She had a solemn look on her face, completely unaware that her neighbor was a monster.

"How long have you lived here?" Brody asked.

"We moved in a couple of years ago," Patricia responded.

Brody wondered if the aunt was still alive. He gripped his phone in one hand and gently squeezed Rebecca's with the other as he thanked Patricia and told her to have a good night.

On closer appraisal of the house, a few of the side windows were boarded. The front room had a window AC unit. The door would be easy to breach. "His aunt might live somewhere else," he said. "She could be nearby. I'm guessing she keeps Jason when Kramer is on the road."

"I can't leave until I know for sure," Rebecca said.

"I know." Brody took that moment to kick the door. It flew open.

Stepping inside, he called for Jason.

There was no response.

It was dark and Brody had no idea what waited inside.

He clicked on a light. The room looked like something out of an episode of *Hoarders*. Stacks of papers and magazines were everywhere. Old pizza boxes and fast-food bags were piled on the coffee table.

Brody caught movement out of the corner of his eye, so he tracked it to the kitchen. "Jason. We're here to help. Your mommy and daddy are looking for you."

A whimper sounded from inside the pantry.

Opening the door slowly, Brody repeated the boy's name.

As light filled the little room, he saw the boy huddled

in the corner. His clothes were dirty and he was frightened. "It's okay, Jason. Take my hand."

The little boy started crying harder.

Rebecca dropped down to her knees. "Hey, Jason. My name is Rebecca and I'm here to take you home. I know a very bad man took you away from your family. He did the same thing to my little brother. It's going to be okay. I know you're scared. But you didn't do anything wrong."

In one swift movement the boy sprang into her open arms, buried his face and cried.

She soothed him, stroking his hair, and when she smiled up at Brody there was a deep sense of peace in her features.

"I'll call his parents first and then the police," he said.

She nodded, moving carefully as if trying not to disturb the boy clinging to her. "Have his parents meet us here. I want to stay until they arrive."

"Absolutely." Brody wouldn't have it any other way.

The Glenns made record time.

As soon as the little boy heard his mother's voice, he broke into a full run toward her. Brody watched Rebecca, witnessed the emotions playing out on her face as each parent thanked her and gave her a hug.

Brody stood back a little, taking it all in. The thought struck him that he'd believed Rebecca to be disloyal. What an idiot he'd been. She was the most loyal sister and advocate that anyone could hope to have in their corner.

As soon as the family walked away, Brody hauled her close to him.

"It all makes sense now," she said, looking into his eyes. "The timing of why Kramer attacked the other morning. He was getting desperate because he must've known I'd found Shane."

"You threatened to expose his lies and uncover the truth. He couldn't have that happen. His life would've been over."

She nodded.

"Are you ready to get out of here?" he asked.

"Yes. Get me away from this."

Brody didn't let go of her hand as they walked away from the house.

She glanced toward the house one more time. "He can't hurt anyone else, Brody. It's over."

THE RIDE BACK to town seemed to zoom by even though neither said much. Brody didn't mind. Silence was comforting as she sat in the middle seat, snuggled next to him, and there was something very right in the world.

Rebecca. *His Rebecca.*

There was a fork in the road ahead. Go left and he'd be taking Rebecca back to her bungalow. Make a right and he'd be heading to his ranch.

The road was split, but his heart knew exactly what it wanted, *if* she wanted him.

He stopped the truck in the middle of the farm road, put on his emergency flashers and opened his door. "Will you step outside with me?"

Surprise was written all over her face, but she did as he said. "Is it safe?"

"Should be at this hour." It was just past midnight. A new day had dawned. Could they make a fresh start?

He met her at the front of the truck, the headlights lighting a path, his heart pounding against his chest. "Rebecca, we can't change the past."

She dropped her gaze to the ground. "I know. And you don't have to say anything, because I already know how you feel."

"Do you?" He lifted her chin until her eyes met his, those intense honey browns vulnerable. "Because I don't think you do. As much as I loved you, I needed to grow up. I had too many wounds from the past, from my mother."

"I'm so sorry about the past, Brody, but I can't change it."

"I wouldn't want you to. We let go of what we had in high school and maybe that was a good thing. Life is crazy and it's uncertain. I'm only sure of about one thing. I love you."

Her eyes sparkled as soon as she heard the words. "I love you, Brody Fields. Always have and I always will. It's only ever been you. But you need more than my words."

He placed his hands around her neck and guided her lips to his, to home. "You're all I need, Rebecca. You're enough."

She kissed him slowly, sweetly; that shy smile had returned.

"I just have one question," he said.

"Which is?"

Right there in the middle of the road, he bent down on one knee, preparing to ask the woman he loved to marry him.

He didn't touch ground before she'd dropped into his arms and said the one word he needed to hear before he had a chance to ask.

"Yes," she said. "I'll be your wife."

Scooping her up, taking her to the passenger side, he

asked the other question on his mind. "You belong at the ranch with me. Are you ready to come home?"

Tears streamed down her beautiful face as she said, "You're home to me, Brody. I'm already there."

Epilogue

"Whatever will I do with one of those things?" Her mother's face screwed up as she motioned toward the laptop Rebecca was setting up on the side table next to her bed. Beside it, she placed Shane's Spider-Man watch.

"Believe me when I say that you're going to want to keep this close," Rebecca said, motioning toward the laptop.

"Tell her I don't know how to use it," Mother said to Brody. Her gaze stopped on the keepsake.

He smiled and his clear blue eyes sparkled. "Trust her. She knows what she's doing."

The past few weeks had been good to her mother after hearing news of Thomas Kramer's death and his aunt's arrest. Her mother had started leaving her room to play chess every afternoon and stopped resisting physical therapy. Every day she was getting stronger and the doctor was hopeful, especially following the initial results of how well her body was adjusting to the new medication.

Rebecca hadn't told her about all the events that had transpired. She'd been waiting for the right moment to talk about Shane. And this was it.

"I'd rather help make wedding plans than dicker around with one of those," Mother protested. Again.

"Just a second." Rebecca pulled up the program she'd installed to allow an overseas face-to-face chat. "There's someone who wants to talk to you."

"What's wrong with the phone? I know mine still has a cord, but people do use it from time to time."

"Nothing. But this call can't be made using one of those." Rebecca checked the screen, her heart thumping in her throat. "Are you there?"

Static and blur were all she had.

Then, the screen cleared up and she saw his face. It was Shane, her baby brother. She'd found him—tests had confirmed it—and she was about to share him with her mother.

Rebecca shifted the laptop so her mother could see. "Mother, it's Shane. He's alive. Your son is alive. And he has something he wants to say to you."

"I heard what happened. How you never gave up on me. I love you, Mom." He looked good, strong.

Her mother clasped her hands together and tears streamed down her face as disbelief transformed into joy. "How could I? You're my baby boy. I love you."

"There's so much I want to know, but I only have a few minutes to talk," Shane said. He had that proud Hughes chin and determined gaze.

"It's okay, son. We have the rest of our lives to get to know each other again." And from the looks of her, her mother planned to stick around to enjoy every moment.

* * * * *

Barb Han's MASON RIDGE *miniseries continues next month. Look for* TEXAS TAKEDOWN *wherever Harlequin Intrigue books and ebooks are sold!*

COMING NEXT MONTH FROM

◆ HARLEQUIN®

INTRIGUE

Available September 15, 2015

#1593 RECKONINGS
The Battling McGuire Boys • by Cynthia Eden
Dr. Jamie Myers has hired fierce ex-SEAL Davis McGuire for protection from her dark past, but she didn't anticipate just how close she would get to her new bodyguard—because Davis is determined to protect Jamie both day...and night.

#1594 HIGH COUNTRY HIDEOUT
Covert Cowboys, Inc. • by Elle James
Wounded ex-soldier Angus Ketchum gets a second chance when he's sent undercover to protect a widowed ranch owner. Angus must rely on his combat skills to keep Reggie and her boy alive—and on his commitment to the mission to keep their attraction in check.

#1595 NAVY SEAL SPY
Brothers in Arms: Retribution • by Carol Ericson
Fresh out of the navy, Liam McCabe's first mission is straightforward—infiltrate then expose the criminal organization Tempest. But then he runs into Katie O'Keefe. Now he's engaged in a high-stakes game of espionage with the one woman who can blow his cover.

#1596 TEXAS TAKEDOWN
Mason Ridge • by Barb Han
Security expert Dylan Jacobs commits to keeping Samantha Turner safe from the Mason Ridge Abductor. But his world nearly crumbles when the villain poses a vicious ultimatum—turn over the woman he loves or never see his beloved daughter again.

#1597 THE AGENT'S REDEMPTION
Special Agents at the Altar • by Lisa Childs
When The Bride Butcher strikes again, FBI agent Jared Bell will stop at nothing to bring closure to the case—including staging an engagement with Rebecca Drummond, the first victim's sister, to lure the madman into a trap...

#1598 THE REBEL • by Adrienne Giordano
Danger ensues when introverted sculptor Amanda LeBlanc partners with David Hennings, the rebellious son of a hotshot defense attorney, to solve a cold case. But will David's desire to fit in with his family risk Amanda's life?

YOU CAN FIND MORE INFORMATION ON UPCOMING HARLEQUIN® TITLES, FREE EXCERPTS AND MORE AT WWW.HARLEQUIN.COM.

HICNM0915

REQUEST YOUR FREE BOOKS!
2 FREE NOVELS PLUS 2 FREE GIFTS!

H HARLEQUIN®

I N T R I G U E

BREATHTAKING ROMANTIC SUSPENSE

YES! Please send me 2 FREE Harlequin® Intrigue novels and my 2 FREE gifts (gifts are worth about $10). After receiving them, if I don't wish to receive any more books, I can return the shipping statement marked "cancel." If I don't cancel, I will receive 6 brand-new novels every month and be billed just $4.74 per book in the U.S. or $5.49 per book in Canada. That's a savings of at least 12% off the cover price! It's quite a bargain! Shipping and handling is just 50¢ per book in the U.S. and 75¢ per book in Canada.* I understand that accepting the 2 free books and gifts places me under no obligation to buy anything. I can always return a shipment and cancel at any time. Even if I never buy another book, the two free books and gifts are mine to keep forever.

182/382 HDN GH3D

Name _____ (PLEASE PRINT) _____

Address _____ Apt. # _____

City _____ State/Prov. _____ Zip/Postal Code _____

Signature (if under 18, a parent or guardian must sign) _____

Mail to the **Reader Service:**
IN U.S.A.: P.O. Box 1867, Buffalo, NY 14240-1867
IN CANADA: P.O. Box 609, Fort Erie, Ontario L2A 5X3
Are you a subscriber to Harlequin® Intrigue books
and want to receive the larger-print edition?
Call 1-800-873-8635 or visit www.ReaderService.com.

* Terms and prices subject to change without notice. Prices do not include applicable taxes. Sales tax applicable in N.Y. Canadian residents will be charged applicable taxes. Offer not valid in Quebec. This offer is limited to one order per household. Not valid for current subscribers to Harlequin Intrigue books. All orders subject to credit approval. Credit or debit balances in a customer's account(s) may be offset by any other outstanding balance owed by or to the customer. Please allow 4 to 6 weeks for delivery. Offer available while quantities last.

Your Privacy—The Reader Service is committed to protecting your privacy. Our Privacy Policy is available online at www.ReaderService.com or upon request from the Reader Service.

We make a portion of our mailing list available to reputable third parties that offer products we believe may interest you. If you prefer that we not exchange your name with third parties, or if you wish to clarify or modify your communication preferences, please visit us at www.ReaderService.com/consumerchoice or write to us at Reader Service Preference Service, P.O. Box 9062, Buffalo, NY 14240-9062. Include your complete name and address.

HI15

⟨H⟩HARLEQUIN®

INTRIGUE

Read on for a sneak preview of
HIGH COUNTRY HIDEOUT, *the next installment of*
COVERT COWBOYS, INC.
by New York Times *bestselling author*
Elle James

*Ranching was Angus Ketchum's first love—until
his last tour of duty shattered that dream. The wounded
ex-soldier gets his second chance when he's recruited
to go undercover to protect widowed ranch owner
Reggie Davis.*

Angus slipped through the wooden rails and waded through the cattle milling around, waiting for the gate to open with the promise of being fed on the other side.

The rider nudged his horse toward the gate and leaned down to open it. Apparently the latch stuck and refused to open. Still too far back to reach the gate first, Angus continued forward, frustrated at his slow pace.

As the horseman swung his leg over to dismount, the gelding screamed, reared and backed away so fast the rider lost his balance and fell backward into the herd of cattle.

Spooked by the horse's distress, the cattle bellowed and churned in place, too tightly packed to figure a way out of the corner they were in.

The horse reared again. Its front hooves pawed at the air then crashed to the ground.

Unable to see the downed cowboy, Angus pushed forward, slapping at the cattle, shoving them apart to make a path through their warm bodies.

Afraid the rider would be trampled by the horse or the cattle, Angus doubled his efforts. By the time he reached him, the cowboy had pushed to his feet.

The horse chose that moment to rear again, his hooves directly over the rider.

Angus broke through the herd and threw himself into the cowboy, sending them both flying toward the fence, out of striking distance of the horse's hooves and the panicking cattle.

Thankfully the ground was a soft layer of mud to cushion their landing, but the cowboy beneath Angus definitely took the full force of the fall, crushed beneath Angus's six-foot-three frame.

Immediately he rolled off the horseman. "Are you okay?"

Dusk had settled in, making it hard to see.

Angus grabbed the man's shoulder and rolled him over, his fingers brushing against the soft swell of flesh beneath the jacket he wore. His hat fell off and a cascade of sandy-blond hair spilled from beneath. Blue eyes glared up at him.

The cowboy was no boy, but a woman, with curves in all the right places and an angry scowl adding to the mess of her muddy but beautiful face. "Who the hell are you, and what are you doing on my ranch?"

Don't miss HIGH COUNTRY HIDEOUT
by New York Times *bestselling author Elle James,*
available October 2015 wherever
Harlequin Intrigue® books and ebooks are sold.

www.Harlequin.com

Copyright © 2015 by Mary Jernigan

Love the Harlequin book you just read?

Your opinion matters.

Review this book on your favorite book site, review site, blog or your own social media properties and share your opinion with other readers!

Be sure to connect with us at:
Harlequin.com/Newsletters
Facebook.com/HarlequinBooks
Twitter.com/HarlequinBooks

HREVIEWS

THE WORLD IS BETTER WITH

Romance

Harlequin has everything from contemporary, passionate and heartwarming to suspenseful and inspirational stories.

Whatever your mood, we have a romance just for you!

Connect with us to find your next great read, special offers and more.

f /HarlequinBooks

🐦 @HarlequinBooks

www.HarlequinBlog.com

www.Harlequin.com/Newsletters

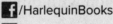 HARLEQUIN®

 A *Romance* FOR EVERY MOOD™

www.Harlequin.com

SERIESHALOAD2015